THE FELL

John Alan

Published by Simon Publishing LLC ®
Simon Publishing LLC is a registered trademark.
https://www.simonpublishingllc.com/

ISBN: 979-8-989 4345-2-7 paperback
ISBN: 979-8-989 4345-3-4 eBook

Library of Congress Control Number: 2023920969

Cover Design by Robin Johnson
        Florida Girl Designs
        www.gobookcoverdesign.com

Printed by Ingram Spark and KDP Amazon

First Edition

6 3 2 1 1 4 9 5 6 0 3 2

The Fell

John Alan

Simon Publishing LLC

Table of Contents

Dedication

To my family, Nancy, Jill, TJ, and Steph

Thank you to the staff at Simon Publishing
Joanne Tailele, Jill Yris and Robin Johnson

Special thanks to my pre-editors
Nancy, TJ, and MaryAnne

Daniel Evan Becket was born to Evette and Marcus Becket. Financially he had wont of nothing while growing up in the New York City area. His father Marcus was a highly successful international broker, dealing in everything from investment properties to shipping. His mother Evette, or Evie to her close friends, was a world-renowned art critic and collector, as well as a very fine artist in her own right. She could also speak four languages perfectly and another three well enough to carry on casual conversations with her many associates around the world. Top that off with her also being the sole heir to a multi-billion-dollar aeronautics and hi-tech manufacturing conglomerate and one has the potential for an ostentatious upbringing for Dan.

However, this was not the case for Dan or Danny as his close friends liked to call him. His mother always called him Daniel, as if to remind him of his sophisticated rearing. Despite all of this well-to-do nonsense, he was fairly well-grounded when it came to taking things for granted. His parents purposely tried to instill in him that the world owed him nothing. They gave him anything he wanted as a child, but to Daniel, the gifts and privileges always seemed to come with a price tag. They expected him to get good grades, excel in sports and act accordingly at all of their many A-list soirees. His parents' expectations became a recipe for the evolution of his acidulous and many times caustic attitude and verbiage.

Grades were not a problem for young Daniel. He eclipsed most of his classmates in many subject areas, especially science and literature. And sports, such as cross country, baseball, basketball and football, came easy to him, but he truly shined the most in swimming, tennis and golf. He wasn't a big fan of tennis or golf, he only played them to appease his father. Still, he learned to eventually hold his own against all of his peers and most of his dad's friends too.

Daniel attended the finest boarding schools in America, England, France and Switzerland. He had a fondness for the three European schools, but he truly enjoyed being in the United States, where his rebellious spirit was much more tolerated. Anyway, his parents were in Europe most of the time, so this situation made it easier for him to get in a little trouble, being they were so far away. He did, however, learn to speak French and German while he was across the Atlantic, a byproduct that made him somewhat appreciate the time he spent there.

His constant traveling as a youth and his parents' constant absence fed Dan's independent thinking. It turned out to be both a blessing and a curse. He developed a strong sense of independence which was often overshadowed by the underlying resentment unfortunately forged in him from being away from his family for so long. His mother had a more flexible schedule than his father and she would visit her son several times during the year, even if for only a day. Daniel appreciated this, but it certainly was not enough to stop him from feeling distant from them.

Daniel's parents wanted him to study business, law or engineering at an Ivy League college in New England. The big expectation was for Daniel to fall in line after graduation and accept a position in either his father's brokerage firm or his maternal granddaddy's military contracted consortium. He would have none of it and sent a clear message to Mom and Pop when he opted to study English Literature and Forensics as a double major undergrad at UCLA.

Dan's true love was to bury himself in the works of Jules Verne, Ernest Hemingway and J.R.R. Tolkien, but that was pretty much the extent of having any real desire to pursue literature as a career. Better to not give in to his family's wishes, piss them off and find his own way in the world.

Marcus Becket was incensed by his only son's perceived betrayal and rewarded his son's tenacity by cutting him off from any of the family's wealth. Although on special occasions, his parents would buy him expensive gifts, they made it quite clear that any monetary or property endowments would not be bestowed upon him until after their deaths or him coming to his senses. The latter, of course, meant that he would have to work for one of their many enterprises; his choice was already no.

This decision meant that Dan would have to pay for college himself. Since his background was one of great wealth, he didn't qualify for any financial aid based on need. He would have to rely on both his academic ability and athletic prowess to garner a scholarship of such magnitude that it would pay for all of his schooling.

What he hadn't realized was that his mother had intervened on his behalf and convinced her husband to relent and pay for their son's education. Evette could have easily financed it herself, but she wanted both a united front with her husband and peace between father and son. Dan didn't know that his mother was working behind the scenes and they didn't know that he had secured a decent scholarship.

When all of this came to light, both sides quietly claimed victory. Mom and Dad saw that their son had taken the initiative and obtained the necessary funds to go to college and felt that by not having to pay for his college allowed them to say that they didn't give in to his rebellious nature, even though they eventually helped with his day-to-day expenses. Dan, on the other hand, felt that by not majoring in a subject of his parents' choosing had shown them that he was his own man. He further proved his point by being a co-captain of his college's swim team and graduating summa cum laude.

He continued his graduate studies at UCLA and completed his master's degree in journalism. Much to his parents' delight, he began a doctorate degree at Princeton. When he unexpectedly left the program to take a job as a local news reporter for a small-time newspaper in Trenton, New Jersey, his parents were livid.

However, Dan did have a true ally in the family. Honorine, his maternal grandmother, was always a loyal supporter. In her 70s, Rina still had a youthful way, was physically fit, remarkably open-minded, and secretly delighted that Dan received his brown hair and blue-eyed good looks from her. She reminded Dan a lot of his mother with her intelligence, style and athleticism, but she was also warm and kind. The only apprehension he held for Rina was that he knew his grandparent's company manufactured weapons, of which he was opposed, another one of his reasons for not jumping aboard and working in the business. Still, he was very close to her and she was always an important influence in his life and would eventually become even more important to him.

Despite the appearance of having a non-forgiving exterior, Dan didn't take himself too seriously. He was raised in the protective bubble of high society, but he never used that as an excuse to explain his occasional inability to play nice with others. As a matter of fact, he was most times embarrassed by his upbringing and went to great lengths not to factor his family's wealth into any equation of his life.

Now, Dan was about to embark on a career-changing assignment and into a way of life that was unknown to most human beings.

1

COLD CASE

hen Dan was called into his editor's office, he expected to get reprimanded for the scuffle that ensued after he had written a news item exposing the afterhours goings-on of a New York City councilman.

As he slipped out of his white 2003 BMW Z4, Dan kept thinking of the kind of professional punishment that would be appropriate for his shoving match with Councilman Jay Spencer outside a Manhattan bar two nights ago. Jay and Roger Harbinger, Dan's managing editor, had been friends for years. They knew each other since college and had kept in touch on and off over the last decade or so. They reconnected seven years ago when Jay was an up and comer in the world of politics and Roger was the assistant editor at his current New York City newspaper, The Metropolitan Observer.

Both sentimentally and critically known as The Mob, the paper had been Dan's home for seven years, was his third newspaper gig and he liked the carte blanche freedom he usually received with his articles. Since he always submitted his work from his laptop, he rarely visited the office.

Maybe I went too far this time, he thought, and now my tail's in a sling. Roger rarely called him into the building and would have never allowed his article on Spencer to be printed in The Mob, hardcopy or online, so ol' Danny Boy decided to give it to Doug Pearson, a professional acquaintance at the New York City Monthly Magazine. Even though Doug took the credit, both Roger and Jay could smell Dan's handiwork.

Dewey's Pub, a favorite watering hole of politicians and the periodical world, held a strange and possibly hostile mix of personnel who infiltrated this establishment, given that reporters enjoyed scorching politicians on their respective front pages. Strong verbal exchanges were welcomed but physical disagreements were almost always avoided or broken up before they could get started. The place served as a sort of demilitarized zone for all of its attendees. Even cops enjoyed a pint or two there on occasion and they generally stayed out of the fray because they were off duty and it would be hard for them to pick a side, since they tended to be a target of both groups.

When Dan opened the door to the pub, Jay crossed an imaginary line when he let loose a right hook towards Dan's jaw. But Dan had plenty of athletic ability left in him. As Jay made his move, Dan's TaeKwonDo training proved invaluable as he moved out of the way of the flying fist and then pinned Jay up against a wall just inside the front door. Bar patrons came from all sides of the room to preserve the sacred no-violence policy of the pub.

Now it was Roger's turn to strike, Dan thought, as he took the elevator up to the fourteenth floor. When the doors opened, he stepped out and stood in the hallway of the newspaper. He felt as though everyone's eyes were on him as if they knew he was DOA. He could hear Jill from the sports department groan as he shuffled his feet past her office. TJ's side-eyed glances from op-ed severed his spine as he grabbed a quick cup of coffee from the breakfast cart. Steph the office manager couldn't even look him straight in the face.

Each time he passed by somebody he nodded and said, "Hey." This futile attempt at pleasantries was not going to garner any support. They all knew what was in store, he thought. He thought wrong. He would later learn that no one had a clue as to what was happening and they could care less. The only things they noticed about him right now was that it looked like he had just rolled out of bed after a night of debauchery, put on a nice sports jacket, a loose tie and then forgot to shave. Dan's imagination was just getting the best of him.

In fact, Dan had always thought that he was more important than he really was. Sure, he was a first-rate reporter, undeniably the best at The Mob, and most likely in the whole city. He couldn't easily be replaced, but Roger would probably replace him without question if he could find a reason that would be appealing to the news outlet's owners.

He strolled up to Roger's secretary's desk and called out, "Hildie, you look beautiful as always!"

The grandmother-aged woman responded with a subtle giggle, but with a more serious tone, she knocked on the door, opened it and said, "Roger. Dan is waiting outside." Then she turned and said, "Okay Dan, go on in." As she walked by him, she giggled again.

Dan looked at her and sensed that it was a foreboding chuckle, if not downright evil-sounding. He paused to collect his thoughts. Does he go in like a frightened puppy or a bulldog with no regrets about the Spencer article? He didn't get a chance to decide as Roger quickly opened the door himself and told him to come in and sit down.

Roger took a seat behind his very large oak desk. Behind that ridiculous monstrosity, he looked far away to Dan, even though they were only a few feet apart. Roger stared intently at him as if he was looking straight through Dan's body and gazing at the framed news articles behind him on the wall. Dan felt uncomfortable, but it was probably because of his late night of liquor and ladies, as opposed to any real fear of Roger.

Finally, after a few unbearable moments, Dan spoke. "So, Roger, what do you got for me?"

Roger continued with his staring as if he was conjuring up a way to say what was on his mind. When he finally did speak, he simply uttered, "Finland."

Dan was confused. Did he hear Roger correctly or did he misunderstand him? Did he say Finland because he was part Finnish or was he leaving on a vacation to visit Finland? Dan casually responded, "Huh?"

Roger then put more words together to form a complete sentence. "I'm sending you to Finland for your next assignment." Dan was again confused. Roger repeated himself and before Dan could protest, he added, "And you leave in two days. This can't wait."

Dan slumped down in his seat with his thoughts reprimanding him. Well, there it is. There's the punishment. It's December. It's freaking cold in New York. It's even more freaking cold in Finland. This is my penance for being the ghostwriter of the Spencer news item.

Dan finally said, "What the hell is this? On what planet do I agree to go to Finland? You've got to be kidding me."

Roger fired back at him. "I'm not kidding. Get your disheveled life in order and fly out of JFK Thursday at 7:30 in the evening."

Dan sat motionless, in shock and couldn't think of a thing to say, which was completely out of character for him. He couldn't tell what he was stunned by the most, not getting a simple reprimand or having to go to Finland.

"Aren't you going to ask me why or for what kind of story?" Roger asked.

"I don't have to," Dan said. "You're sending me to Neverland as a way of getting back at me for the Spencer article."

Roger gave him a perplexed look and responded, "What Spencer article? I never assigned you to do a piece on Jay Spencer."

Dan could feel the temperature in the room drop. Roger directed the conversation back to Finland. "Investigate an unsubstantiated story about a strange phenomenon that may or may not be occurring in a remote region in the northeastern part of the country."

Dan said, "Remote region? The whole damn country's a remote region."

Roger continued as if he was never interrupted. "We don't have a lot of details yet, but it's opening the eyes of certain individuals over there and in other countries and I want you to take a look."

Dan asked, "Why aren't their authorities looking into this? How about their military or even news people? We could send our CIA. I'm not a cop or a spy. I'm just a reporter."

Roger chose his next words carefully. "You're maybe one of the best around at what you do." Dan was caught off guard. A compliment from Roger was rare and not his style. "Besides, we can't officially send a government rep in without an invitation, which we do not have. They will allow the press in to do fluff pieces about their country, however, and you're our choice. You're going there on the pretense that you're writing an article about the holidays in Finland."

Dan tried to interrupt him. "Fluff? Roger this is 2019. There's no way in hell I'm doing fluff anymore."

Roger ignored him and continued, "Also, the area in question borders Russia and even though our government must be drooling about putting one over on those guys, I'm pretty certain that the Pentagon doesn't want to risk an international incident. Both countries are still tense over Russia annexing Crimea and continuing to push its weight around in Ukraine. Our government does not want to give them a reason to swarm their border with Finland, thinking we're up to something. The fact that there may be some kind of supernatural connotation attached to this mystery would not sit well with any authorities, no matter which country was involved."

"Supernatural connotation?" Dan asked. "You are joking, right?"

Roger held a piece of paper in one hand, looked Dan in the eyes and responded, "Not kidding. Our contacts on the ground have said that for many years there have been circumstances that can't be explained in a national park called, um, let's see, uh, Urho Kekkonen. There are no towns or villages anywhere near the part of the park in question. There are, however, various settlements in and around it on both sides of the border near a landmark known in Finland as the Korvatunturi Fell."

Dan asked, "Fell?"

Roger kept going. "These settlements, if you can even call them that, consist of people whose families have owned homes for centuries. They are of very modest means, even quite poor in some cases. They accept very little to no assistance from either country's government. Also, they are not the ones complaining that something weird is going on. In fact, they haven't been very cooperative in the past when questioned by local Finnish or Russian police. Many of them live in such remote areas that the cops don't even bother traveling there. We're talking hundreds of miles or kilometers away from the nearest city."

"You mentioned something about contacts being on the ground. What contacts?" Dan asked.

Roger paused briefly. "Pete from regional news, who was born there, was visiting family in a small city called Rovaniemi, which is probably the nearest city to your eventual destination. People he knows came across some very unusual occurrences. He called me and so I called you. He and his team are your main boots on the ground and they're waiting for you."

Dan asked, "Why wasn't the assignment given to Pete? After all, you said that Pete was born in Finland. He's already there and has a team in place. He could probably write fluff as well as anyone."

Roger replied, "Pete has no international reporting experience and isn't an investigative reporter either. Although his writing is good with a keen eye for details, he's not a lion like you. Pete's comfort zone is the tri-state area. Remember, the pretense is fluff, but it's not the true nature of it. That's why we need someone with investigative skills."

Roger knew that Pete could be very useful for this particular venture; he knew the culture and spoke the local language, plus Russian. Even though most Finns spoke some English, many in the back region did not. The excursion would take them to the outskirts of a small town called Savukoski where some of Pete's relatives lived and could provide accommodations for Dan.

Dan wanted to continue arguing about going, but he knew he had no case. Realizing this, he stood and started towards the door. As he was turning the knob, Roger said, "Look, I know you have reservations about going. I'm sending you on this assignment because you're a damn good investigator." Dan nodded, pulled the door open and as it closed behind him, he heard Roger shout, "And because of the Jay Spencer article."

He stood outside the door. Hildie walked over and calmly handed him an envelope that included an itinerary sheet and plane ticket details, along with his expense account information.

"Good luck," she said.

Dan grinned and nodded a silent thank you. He then walked through the outer office door and became consumed with one thought. What's a fell?

2

PETE, NANCY, &

MORE COMPANY

The Pete that Roger made reference to was Pete Sironen, who had just recently finished his third year in the employment of The Mob. Pete loved to call the Observer by its nickname. It never got old to answer someone about where he was employed. He would respond to them by saying, "I work for The Mob!" And then he would laugh as if he used that line for the very first time.

While in Finland visiting family, he took an overnight trip to a small town called Sodankyla. He then proceeded to travel to the smaller town of Savukoski where his Finnish cousins owned a cabin that had been in the family for about two hundred years. Technically, Pete was part owner too because he and his cousins Aleksi, Arturo and Jaako had inherited it from their shared grandparents, who were still alive and living reasonably close to the fell.

Pete was born in the little Finnish village of Saariselka. His parents moved to the United States when he was a boy and he had only been back to visit a few times in the last ten years. His cousins, mainly Jaako, maintained the property in Savukoski and he helped financially with the cabin's upkeep. After all, it was a couple of centuries old and throughout the years, some of it was torn down and rebuilt in order to keep it relatively modern. It still managed to keep its old-world glory. Except for the solar powered electricity and indoor plumbing, the cabin looked like it could make the cover of Pioneer Living, if there was such a magazine. Pete also put in extra money because his cousins openly accused him of being a wealthy American and that appeared to make him feel guilty enough to chip in more. He was tired of hearing the annoying comments from his cousins. "Look at the rich American. Must be nice to be rich."

His cousins spoke perfect English, as could a majority of people in that beautiful country. This meant that they could easily banter with him. They called him Pez, because the anagram PEZ came from his full name Pietari Erik Zachrisson Sironen. He was named after one of his great-grandfathers, Pietari Erik Zachrisson-Kurtti, a half Finnish and half Swedish banker.

His cousins always teased him because he had Americanized his first name, which is why, he in turn, Americanized theirs. In any given situation you would hear someone yell, "Pez. Hey Pez!" This would soon be followed by, "Yeah Jake? Yeah Alex? Yeah Artie?"

Dan and Pete knew each other a bit more than just casually. They crossed paths on several occasions while on the job and had even shared information at least a few times. They also had a common acquaintance in one Doug Pearson from the Jay Spencer fiasco.

Dan now started thinking about other things such as getting packed for an indefinite trip. He wanted to make sure his apartment was checked on occasionally and, of course, there was Frank Burns or FB for short. FB, a rat terrier, was Dan's pride and joy. Actually, FB was a female, but Dan loved the name because of his obsession with the television show *MASH,* which was off the air before he was even born.

He thought the funniest character was Frank Burns. His father Marcus loved the sitcom and the two of them would watch reruns together, on occasion, when Dan was much younger. It was one of Dan's few favorite memories about his dad. FB hadn't been treated kindly by nature when it came to looks, but she was smart, sweet and affectionate. Everyone who met her loved her instantly.

Dan finally entered his apartment and FB immediately ran to him and jumped all over the place as if he had been gone for a year. It had only been ten hours. "Hello little one," he said.

Shortly thereafter, came a knock at the door and Dan knew who it was before even answering it. He yelled, "Coming!"

He opened the door and there stood his next-door neighbor Nancy. She was FB's caretaker when Dan was working and he thought the dog sometimes loved her more than him. After all, he was gone a lot and Nancy would keep the dog at her apartment when he was at work. She worked at home on her computer for a software development company and was easily able to care of the little critter. She would drop the dog off at his place by six o'clock in the evening unless he called to tell her that he would be later. If she didn't hear him come in by nine, she would grab the dog and keep it with her until he did finally get home. She would drop by when he got in, just to give an update on the dog, but also because she had feelings for him. This was her way of spending time with him even though most days it was only for a few minutes. She was pretty, intelligent and an interesting conversationalist.

Dan liked her too. He was just too hesitant to move to the next level with her for fear that it could ruin their friendship, if the relationship went south. He kept irregular hours on an average day and was away a great deal of time for days and sometimes even weeks. His schedule was a hindrance and his temperament could also be a deterrent for a successful courtship.

Still, they would go out for an occasional coffee and sometimes watch a little TV together. Nancy spent a great deal of time at home working six days a week and did not have the energy to put into a real relationship. She would have an occasional date, as did Dan, but they rarely discussed the topic with one another. It was almost as if they were trying to spare each other's feelings even though they really didn't need to be that considerate. They were officially just friends, but had a connection that transcended it being just a simple friendship.

They chatted it up a bit before Dan informed her of his latest excursion. He asked, "How was the little floor duster?"

"Great and adorable as always." She started to sense that this small talk meant that she would probably be taking care of the little lady again. It always meant that.

Dan said, "That's good. Hey, that's actually great. Thank you again for watching her, for always watching her."

She didn't mind watching FB. It would get her out of the house when she took her for a walk, usually to Central Park, which was several blocks away but not far enough to make either lose their breath. The trip back, however, was a different story. Nancy usually ended up carrying the tiny package home.

She loved her time with FB and even though she never mentioned it to Dan, the dog served a greater purpose. The dog's unusual appearance would give guys the courage to begin talking to her when they might otherwise feel intimidated by her striking good looks. Nancy didn't need FB for dates, but she wasn't the type to initiate a conversation with men she had just met.

Dan turned briefly away from Nancy to put his work bag down. He stood and looked at her. She waited for him to ask if she would take care of the dog while he was away.

He opened his mouth and began to say, "Nance, I was wondering…"

She eagerly said, "Yes."

"You don't even know what I was going to ask you."

"I know exactly what you were going to ask." The real question for Nancy was for how long. "How many days this time?"

The best he could tell her was, "Not sure. I could be gone for several weeks and I'm leaving in two days. If it's okay, I will drop FB off on Thursday around three in the afternoon."

Always before they parted ways, they would both pause and lock eyes as if they wanted to spill their guts about how they really felt about one another. But this time, just like every other time, they both ended the conversation with a melancholy, "Goodbye."

3

THE ICELAND COMETH

The two days flew by and Dan found himself in an Uber on his way to the airport. He had said his goodbyes to FB and Nancy. He hated doing it. He hated leaving the little rodent again, even though he knew she was in good hands. FB didn't seem to mind at all, but he felt that he didn't deserve her in his life, or Nancy for that matter. Before he could give any more thought to it, the car pulled up to the Icelandair sign and the driver said, "We're here."

Dan headed inside. He checked his bags and after going into the main part of the airport, he headed through security. The airport didn't seem as crowded as it usually was when he flew at this time of the day. He was happy because he cruised through security without a hitch. He needed something to feel good about because of the long road ahead of him.

The plan was that Dan would land in Iceland at around six in the morning and have a nine-

17

ty-minute layover at Keflavik Airport in Reykjavik before heading to Helsinki and landing there at around one in the afternoon, Helsinki time. He would then have another layover for over three hours before arriving in the small city of Rovaniemi on Finnair shortly before four-thirty that afternoon. The time of arrival didn't concern Dan as much as it normally would. Iceland and Finland were either in or close to the arctic circle. The amount of sunlight was minimal during the winter months and with the freezing temperatures, Dan could care less about what part of the day he landed.

Pete Sironen and maybe one or all of his cousins would pick him up. They would then bring him to the cabin, which was a few hours away. This was if everything went according to schedule. Needless to say, Dan would be absolutely exhausted after this part of his ordeal was over.

Dan found a seat about thirty feet from the gate and collapsed into it. He grabbed his air pods and checked the playlist on his phone. He liked to listen to Kane Brown among other modern country artists. If he went old school country, he usually chose Johnny Cash. If he decided on vintage rock, it was a toss-up between Carlos Santana or Bruce Springsteen. He would occasionally listen to old rhythm and blues to the likes of Little Walter and Muddy Waters. Early blues Elvis was okay too. Much of this was due to his parents, but he liked all of it anyway. He settled on listening to his secret guilty pleasure, Norah Jones. He kept this on the down low because if any of his male friends found out, he would be crucified by their ruthless comments.

He closed his eyes and drifted in and out of consciousness as he slumped down in his seat. He had thought about learning a few catchphrases in Finnish and reading about the culture, but he was too slothful to bother. He was lucky that the Finns were more acquainted with American culture and the English language than most Americans realized. A large majority of Americans ashamedly had little to no knowledge of Finland.

Dan awoke to the sounds and shufflings of a young man attempting to get to a seat right next to him. Dan was in a seat near a window and had hoped that he would remain undisturbed until boarding. Dan shifted to his right to face the window. He was at first annoyed and stunned that someone would sit near him when there were clearly so many empty seats all around him. As he became more coherent, Dan realized that he had been asleep longer than he had thought and that there weren't too many seats near the gate left. The place was pretty well stacked with people and the idea that the boy would sit three feet away was not too unreasonable.

The youngster looked to be anywhere from a preteen to a mid-aged teenager. Dan couldn't really tell because he had no frame of reference. He didn't know too many children. He had a goddaughter who was six years old, the product of two old college friends. Other than that, he was clueless as to how to communicate with anyone under the age of twenty. This child was not big in stature. He was thin and the approximate size of an average fourteen- to fifteen-year-old, but he had a much more youthful looking face than that. He also had a gaze of wonderment as if he was scoping out the world around him for the first time. The kind of gaze a five-year-old has after Santa brought presents on Christmas Eve.

Dan heard the young prepubescent-sounding voice of the almost-man ask him, "Do you mind if I sit here?" The questioner looked at Dan with round eyes and remained a few feet away from him as if he was expecting to be shooed away.

Dan nodded and softly said, "No. Go ahead."

The young passenger tried to find a way to start a conversation. Dan shifted his slunken body to allow the newcomer more room to get comfortable in his seat. There was a seat between them but it wasn't enough distance for Dan. He turned away to subliminally hint to the boy that he did not want to be disturbed.

The trespasser dropped his bags hard on the ground and it made Dan jump. He sat down. He said to anyone who would listen, "I'm so glad that I'm not too late."

There was still plenty of time before passengers would board. The adolescent only lasted a few minutes before he struck up a conversation with an unwilling Dan. Dan put the air pod back in his ear that he had removed when the boy first spoke to him. He was attempting to go back to his music, but was quickly interrupted again by the intruder's question.

The boy asked, "Are you listening to music?"

Dan nodded yes.

The boy rambled on with, "I like classic rock and classical music such as Bach, Tchaikovsky and Mozart. I really like classic rock artists that have classical music influences like Electric Light Orchestra, Trans-Siberian Orchestra and Queen."

Dan softly mouthed the words, "ELO? Queen?" *Is this kid over fifty?* He remembered that his own father loved ELO.

"Where are you going?" the youngster asked.

Dan answered, "Finland." Then he turned away from the inquisitive youth as if he had just hung out a *Do Not Disturb* sign.

"I'm going to Iceland," the boy said without being asked. "I can't tell you why because I don't really know myself. I just know that I have to be there by today."

Dan's interest in this conversation went from a zero to at least a three after hearing this. He was a bit amused that the boy was going to a unique destination like Iceland by himself and didn't know why. Dan asked him his name.

He replied, "Thad...uh…Ted or Teddy Wintermi…uh…Winters."

Dan was now sitting up in his seat with his interest starting to increase even more. Dan's investigative reporter intuition was starting to kick into a higher gear. This Ted or whoever he was, acted as if he didn't want to give his real name. Dan went from being annoyed to carrying on a conversation that lasted through the boarding process and into their airplane seats.

Dan and Ted, by amazing happenstance, were seated in the same row with an empty seat in between them. Dan began offering a few table scraps of his life. "I'm a reporter on assignment in Finland."

Ted said, "Finland and its people are actually known as Suomi to the Finns."

Dan often wondered why the country's athletic teams always had that word on their jerseys, instead of Finland. He never thought to investigate it out of sheer laziness or just plain apathy. He was intrigued by Ted, Teddy or Thad. Dan wondered if he was a runaway. He thought maybe he was hiding some deep dark secret, not the skeleton-in-the-closet kind, but one that was still very important to him or his family. Dan did not have a clue as to how close he actually was about this or if he was close at all. He hoped he would find out soon and that it just hadn't presented itself yet.

Having Ted next to him made the trip bearable from takeoff to landing. He thought he was going to sleep through everything, but this tyke was damn interesting. His parents were loaded.

Ted said, "My mother and father are archaeologists. They have written books and given lectures about their adventures around the world and periodically teach courses at the college level. They are also shrewd business people who made a fortune through various investments and had donated money to a number of colleges and causes in the Americas, Europe and Africa. They're away from home a lot, but I have a great support unit of family and friends to take care of me."

Dan could identify with most of what Ted was experiencing. Ted was an only child, but he did not seem spoiled in the least. He was quite a talker but he appeared to be the type of individual who liked to listen to what other people were saying. It was as if he was absorbing what everyone was communicating, even if it was something mundane. Dan watched as Ted conversed with a flight attendant. He made it seem as though she had the most important information in the world and that he needed to know all about it or he would die.

Ted went on to give Dan a complete biography of his life. After all, they had several hours to kill and there was no way to stop him from talking anyway. Ted said, "I have lived all over the world with my parents and relatives."

He chose his words carefully even when he appeared to be just blurting them out. He was so outgoing in a way that might strike a person as being much too forward. Dan likened it to a person who was so intelligent that he couldn't get the words out fast enough before more ideas popped into his head.

He sounded a tad English, but he wasn't, probably due to his upper crust New England rearing. He said, "I've lived mainly in Boston in Beacon Hill."

Dan always felt that rich Bostonians were the last vestige of any linguistic connection to England. Ted's family had one of the most expensive houses in the Beacon Hill section of the city.

Ted said, "My parents and I vacation most summers on Martha's Vineyard or Cape Cod, where we own houses. When school is in session, I attend boarding school."

Dan surmised that he probably often showed off his intelligence in boarding school, but not in a condescending way. It was easy to see that he was likely a serious student and yet he had a childish goofiness that probably kept him well grounded.

His parents Ted and Ellinor, or Ellie for short, traveled the world and Ted would join them whenever he could. His father was a silent partner in a worldwide electronics firm and his mother was the CEO and part owner of a large import/export business. They were constantly on the go, but both businesses were based out of London and Hong Kong, making it convenient for Ellie and the older Ted to travel together.

Despite the frequent separation, they were a close-knit family. Young Ted said to Dan, "I am never truly alone even when I appear to be on my own. We have a loyal English gentleman on retainer to oversee all of my affairs."

Dan laughed when he heard young Winters say the word retainer, but the boy was only telling the truth. According to Ted, this man always lived near Ted wherever his education took him. When Ted traveled, this gentleman would be with him. Dan was suspicious as to where this assistant was right now, but he never asked Ted.

"His name is Artemis Trent," Ted continued. "I really know very little about his personal life, except that he has been an employee of my family for at least a decade. My parents consider Trent to be more of a friend or family member, rather than being on their payroll." Ted considered him to be his closest friend and confidante, but Trent kept his own private affairs just that, private.

Ted's parents knew more about him than they would let on and Ted told Dan that every time he asked them for a little information about Artemis, all they would say was that he grew up in northern England, he had two sisters and that he led a quiet life working in some insurance corporation. Despite being a man of mystery, Ted loved and trusted him as much as he did his parents.

Their plane was just about to go into its final hour of flight when Dan got up to use the restroom. As he made it to the door, it opened and a finely dressed man in an expensive suit stepped out and paused. He quickly looked Dan up and down before moving out of the way. Dan also paused because he suddenly got a slight shiver up and down his spine. The kind of shiver he would get when he knew something was not quite right. He watched the man sit down a few rows behind his and Ted's seats before he himself entered the tiny restroom.

Dan had been a reporter for nearly ten years and every once in a while, he would get that weird thought or feeling that something was out of place. This was one of those times. He finished up and made his way to his seat knowing that he would have to walk by this person of interest. As he passed, he took a quick glance and found that the man's eyes were focused on him like laser beams. Dan turned quickly away. When he got to his seat, Ted immediately continued his conversation as if Dan had never left.

He began again about his family and said, "I'm of Dutch, German, Danish, English, Irish, Scottish and Welsh descent on my father's side. My mother is mostly French with some Italian and a bit of North African, Middle Eastern and Asian to round out my very eclectic genetic background."

Dan could only respond with, "I see." Then he tried to look over his shoulder with no success.

Then Ted added, "Oh and I have some Iberian in me, but my DNA test couldn't decide whether it was Portuguese or Spanish blood or both."

To look at him, you could definitely see the western European in this walking and constantly talking United Nations. He was somewhat fair-skinned, but his facial features suggested a Mediterranean influence, which could be any of the regions from the Iberian Peninsula to western Asia.

His family spoke many languages other than English. Spanish, French, Dutch, Arabic, German, Italian, Chinese, Japanese with a touch of Korean and Hebrew for good measure were spoken with some regularity depending on which business associates they were communicating with. His father could also get by when conversing in all of the Scandinavian languages and would freely insert them all into one conversation to the point where he had forgotten which language he was speaking. This would confuse his business associates at times, but they politely refrained from laughing or saying anything condescending.

Ted knew a little of every one of these languages, but he was particularly well versed in French and Spanish due to the tutelage of his mother. He was currently learning Chinese and Portuguese at school.

He liked to watch and participate in all kinds of sports. He competed in track at school and was learning self-defense and parkour like his mother. He also played several instruments such as guitar, violin, piano and drums. Dan wondered how this wizard-like phenom had the time and stamina to fit in all of his schooling, music lessons, language learning and sports into his relatively short life. Dan surmised that his brain must be the size of a watermelon.

Ted finished with the long dissertation of his life and finally got around to asking Dan about his. "So, Dan, can you tell me something about you?"

Knowing that their flight was soon ending, Dan kept his bio much shorter, but Ted listened quite intently and stopped him many times to ask questions. Dan sensed his genuineness and gladly gave up information about his job, FB, his family background and even his friendship with Nancy. After all, he figured that he would never see Ted again, so what was the harm? Ted then said something that hit Dan in a strange way.

He said, "Don't waste time. Do the things that you've been neglecting. That includes Nancy. You never know when it's going to be too late."

This sounded as if Ted was expunging prophecies. Dan found this eerie because after Ted had said it, he stopped talking, faced forward and just stared. All Dan could muster up in response was, "Sounds reasonable."

This was not the only thing that got Dan thinking. Much earlier in their talk, Ted was going through a list of the schools that he had attended in his lifetime. He said the word *Wickets*, but then he stuttered after saying it as if he had given up too much information and then regretted it. Dan's investigative mind jumped all over that faux pas.

He hoped that Ted would see the need to use the restroom so that he could sneak a peek at the internet and look up the word Wickets, Wicketts or whatever.

When the time finally did come, Dan worked fast but came up empty. There was no website and no news items, as if it didn't exist. His need-to-know mind led him to email his oldest childhood friend in Boston, Joe Archer, about both Ted and Trent. The text read, "Archer. What do you know about a private boarding school near Boston called Wickets? Not sure of the spelling."

Joe Archer had once worked for the *Boston Globe* before giving it all up and opting instead to pursue a career in the CIA, although he was no longer with the CIA. Dan guessed that it was because Archer had been reprimanded too many times by his government superiors. He seemed to have a difficult time balancing his earlier world of broadcasting information and his more recent world of suppressing information. Dan figured that Archer was still somehow connected to the world of espionage, but he refrained from giving out any details. He was officially the owner of a private security company and right now he was Dan's only hope at knowing the scoop about Ted.

Dan's second email message to him said, "Need info on a Ted Winters and Englishman named Artemis Trent."

Joe always teased Dan about getting a real reporting job at a more famous newspaper like the *New York Times*, the *Chicago Tribune* or the *Boston Globe*. Dan always laughed it off, but not-so-deep-down, he had always thought about it, but he was a New York City boy at heart. He would donate his soul to work at the *Times,* hoping that it would still be in existence by the time he had a chance to be employed there.

He had the credentials, experience and articles to be considered. He put out a few feelers to see if he had a chance at a job there like his current one, but the responses were always negative.

"You'll sometimes have to report on public interest stories," the interviewers would say to him.

To Dan, this meant that they would be fluff pieces and be a slap in the face to him. He hadn't done fluff since his first year in the business. He went right into hard local news and then national news within a three-year span. He went international in his sixth year, but he preferred staying local. He loved investigative work that involved exposing bad cops, crooked politicians or illegal business transactions.

Because he did sometimes work internationally, he was the cream of the crop of reporters. At least in his own mind he was. It was this arrogance that gave Dan the tendency to get argumentative when he either didn't get the assignment he wanted or had received one that he hated. He agreed that he was cranky and argumentative at times, but arrogant? Never! Even though he was a cranker, he never refused an assignment. He just liked to give Roger a hard time.

He was now waiting for Archer to reply. Archer's response came rather quickly and Dan didn't get the answer he wanted. After a few jovial knock downs of Dan's character, he got serious and his text said, "Never heard of the school, Winters or Trent." He gave Dan some hope when he also said, "Will contact a friend in D.C."

It was quite strange that the school's name didn't pop up anywhere on paper or on the internet. Everything was on the internet and this made a red flag go up in the minds of both men. The only other explanation was that Ted was lying, but Dan didn't want to believe that. He remembered the way Ted reacted when he said Wickets and then stumbled past it.

Archer's response had come just in time. Ted came back and because of his extreme desire to know everything that was going on around him, he would have most likely asked Dan what was going on with his texting. The plane was descending and everyone strapped in for the landing. Ted continued to talk, but at this moment Dan didn't mind. He didn't like landing even though he had done it hundreds of times.

It was only when Ted started talking about airline statistics and said, "The chances of crashing upon landing are…"

Dan ignored the rest of Ted's sentence. Dan became unraveled for a moment until he looked over at Ted and saw such a sense of innocence on the teenager's face. Dan recognized that this innocence, in its own way, probably blocked most cowardice and stress from invading Ted's thoughts. He was brave because he was too naive to think that bad things happen a great deal of the time.

Dan wished that he himself had even a tiny slice of this left in his own mind. Innocence lost, he thought. This is how Dan had summed up his own life. What a great name for a book that he could write. Then it came to him. That ship had sailed. It had been done already. He wasn't even in elementary school when a novel of that name came out in bookstores. Pretty good book, he recalled, when he was old enough to read it.

Dan started to realize that he had been acting a bit squirrelly. It was the seemingly snail's pace of a landing that was driving him loony. He snapped out of it when he heard the ding of his phone informing him that he had received a text. He looked over at Ted to see that he was preoccupied with looking out the window at the dark sky. Dan snuck a quick peek at his phone and saw that it was Archer. He hit the text with his thumb and saw the message. "Call me ASAP."

The plane finally hit the runway and after an eternity, it finally came to a stop. Dan gave out a sigh and Ted proclaimed, "Well, we stayed within the odds. We made it out alive!"

After a few moments, people stood and started to retrieve their carry-ons; most didn't wait for the seatbelt light to go off. Dan got up to get his bag from the overhead compartment and saw Ted's backpack with patches from around the world plastered all over it. He remembered Ted had it strapped to his back earlier. As he went to grab it for Ted, a hand came out of nowhere and locked around his wrist. Dan turned and saw that it was the finely suited man with the laser beam eyes. "I'll get that," the man said.

Dan didn't protest. Even though he was put off by this, Dan thought there was nothing to gain by getting into a squabble with a guy who looked like he was in his sixties. Dan released his hand from Ted's pack and the man promptly let go of his wrist.

Ted, seeing the astonishment on Dan's face, said to him, "Don't worry. This is my assistant and mentor Artemis Trent."

Dan tentatively extended his hand and said, "Sorry and hello. My name is Dan Becket, Mr. Trench."

Dan was met with, "It's not Trench you pillock, it's Trent!"

That was Dan's cue to turn, grab his own luggage and start walking. He couldn't wait to get away from the man. As he left the plane, he wondered why this fellow had only revealed himself after the flight was over and done with. It was also very strange that Ted never mentioned him being a few rows back. It made no sense. If his parents felt the need to have a bodyguard hovering over him, then that meant they were concerned for his well-being. They were wealthy beyond belief and could easily charter or even buy their own jet. This would have insured his safety much more than being on a public flight.

All of these thoughts were crazily swirling around in Dan's head. His intuitiveness was rushing to the surface at warp speed. Seeing that he would probably never cross paths with the two again, he decided to let it go. After all, he had other things like Finland on his mind. That was until he heard Ted yell to him, "Hey Dan! Wait up! You didn't say goodbye!"

Dan slowed down and waited for Ted to catch up to him. He put a string of questions together that made him sound a little like Ted. "I gotta ask," Dan said. "Why the hired hand? Why not get your own plane? It would be a lot safer since somebody feels the need for you to be protected. Actually, why do you need protection? Is it because of your parents' money?"

Ted smiled as they were about to go in different directions. This sudden interrogation made him laugh a little. He thought about how he might respond to this battery of pop quiz questions. "I fly on planes because I enjoy the company and conversation. If I was on my own plane, there wouldn't be any interesting people to talk to." He looked over at Trent and uttered, "Sorry Artemis. I didn't mean that you aren't interesting. It's just that I can talk to you anytime. I don't get out much except to meet up with my parents. I want to meet new faces and find out more about what's going on in the world."

All three of them stopped when they realized that they were at the end of the line for their little group. Ted reached out to shake Dan's hand. Dan reacted in the same way. "It's been both interesting and a pleasure meeting you," Ted said.

"The pleasure has also been mine," Dan said. "You're quite an interesting young man and I see only good things coming your way in life."

Ted shifted his weight and with a nervous grin towards Trent, he then said, "Thank you. Can I look you up someday at *The Observer*? It's probably easier for me to find you rather than you finding me."

Dan found that statement rather odd for Ted to say, but he replied, "Sure. Why not? I'd be interested in finding out what trails you blazed in the world!"

Dan gave him a last wave and quickly glanced in Trent's direction. He nodded but Trent just stared back with no emotion. As the three parted ways, Dan walked away with a lot of uncertainty. Who was this Trent guy anyway? Can I kick his ass? I think I can. No. I know I can. I'm in good shape. I'm young. Well, I'd give him a good fight.

Dan turned around to size up his competition once again and realized that Trent and Ted weren't heading for the outside of the airport. They were quickly walking towards Juneyao Airlines, which was a Chinese carrier. He was dumbfounded. The thought of something being out of place went through his mind again. He stopped walking. He stared at all of the people scurrying to their destinations and shrugged. Why get all worked up over this? I'll probably never see him again and I certainly don't need to see that paid goon again. Ever again. Then he subduedly muttered out loud, "What the hell is a pillock?"

4

WICKED GOOD

It finally hit him that he was supposed to have called Joe Archer as soon as possible. He walked to an area of the airport where he could have a private conversation and sat down. He moved his bags near his feet and called him.

Archer's first words were, "What took you so long?" He got right to the point. "Wickets is a highly secretive and exclusive school for young people."

"So, what's the big deal? And why all of the internet secrecy?" Dan asked.

Archer snapped back, "Put a lid on it for a second. It's secret to the point where it doesn't even exist. Well, not officially. It's so secret that it's on an island in Boston Harbor and nobody knows it's there. There's even a more secluded location on an island in Buzzards Bay off the southern coast of Massachusetts. My buddy in D.C. was only able to get me any intel on this because he's not in the CIA anymore. He got an upgrade to another agency that doesn't exist to the American taxpayer. He couldn't and wouldn't give me that agency's name or he'd have to kill me. And then I'd have to kill you."

"Wait. What?" Dan dumbfoundedly asked.

"You know what I mean," Archer said, realizing his mistake. "This new friend of yours is or was enrolled in a school for individuals with enhanced abilities or at least with the potential to have them."

Dan scoffed. "Enhanced abilities? Are you saying that our government is involved with a school that trains young minds to do things with their so-called superpowers? Is this like the Soviet Cold War programs that dealt with remote spying?"

Archer scoffed right back. "I didn't say Wickets was run by the government. In fact, my contact and I don't know who or what actually runs it. He's not even sure about the origin of the school's name, which is actually spelled W-I-C-K-I-T. He came up with only two possibilities. John W. Wickit was a Bostonian of little or no fame who was a local bookstore owner in the eighteenth century. His shop specialized in books on the occult and other supernatural topics. This was unheard of back in the day and extremely dangerous, given the venomous religious extremists that lived in Massachusetts way back then. His store was burned to the ground by local zealots who branded his establishment a den of the devil. The only other theory my spy had was much simpler and rather silly."

"Silly?" Dan asked.

"Yes," Archer replied. "My contact's other thought based on his findings, is that the school's name is just a play on words for the often-used word in Boston lingo, wicked. The word sounds like wickit when used by some people there and it pretty much is used to emphasize all kinds of words. Wickit good. Wickit evil. Wickit anything. I say the first explanation makes more sense."

Dan mulled over Archer's findings for a few moments and thought about two things. He was curious about the kind of abilities Ted Winters may have and whether he was using these abilities, given the confusing nature of his plane ride to Iceland and then China.

Archer then added. "FYI Dan. We did the remote spying back in the day too!" He also threw some more astounding info at Dan. "That older gentleman who accompanied your boy, you know the one called Trent. Well, he isn't just an assistant to the kid. His actual name is Archibald Butterly and he's no common bodyguard. He's former or maybe even current MI6, as in British Intelligence, as in James Bond, as in super spy. Oh, and your little friend isn't who he said he was. His name is really Thaddeus Wintermint II."

Dan jumped in. "What do these Harry Potter characters have to do with anything?"

Archer laughed. "Don't you know the Wintermint name?"

Dan chuckled. "Yeah. It's the name of a chewing gum."

Archer quickly corrected him. "No. It's the name of a wealthy businessman. Thaddeus Wintermint I is involved in all kinds of companies around the world. His wife too. They are also renowned researchers and archaeologists. Your new buddy, Thaddeus Wintermint II, is some kind of boy genius who is supposedly able to predict future events and is quite nimble on his feet. Trent was once a government sponsored assassin and special attaché assigned to keep British dignitaries safe at all costs, including members of the royal family."

Dan should have been completely overwhelmed by all that he had just heard but he wasn't, not totally. His first thought was that he'd never be able to kick Trent's ass, giving the man's spy pedigree. Once he got his train of thought back on track, he wondered how he was ever going to process all of this and still focus on Finland.

He asked, "How did your government snoop come upon all of this info?"

Archer replied, "I don't know. My contact also knew that Pete Sironen was already in Finland and that you're on your way to meet up with him. By the way Dan, do not tell your editor about all of this. The fewer people who know, the better."

Dan now started to wonder if Roger knew anything about any of this. Did he know about the feds being aware of his assignment? Was he cooperating with them or was he just an ignorant stooge who was unknowingly involved with international intrigue? Maybe it was just a coincidence. Dan opted for the ignorant stooge idea. He thanked his old friend. Before he could say anything else, he realized that Archer had abruptly ended their phone call.

Archer in turn, did not want to keep talking for fear that he might slip up and give Dan too much information about his covert comrade. He thrived on having a James Bond type ally and he wanted to keep him in the shadows. If his contact's identity was ever revealed, he could be killed by enemies of the country or even by his own people. Archer could also be killed and Dan too. Archer couldn't take any chances. Unfortunately, he would never hear from his James Bond again.

5

BOB VILA WOULD BE DISAPPOINTED

After an hour had passed, Dan was on the second plane of his journey. He wondered if anyone would be sitting next to him and if that person would be as strangely entertaining as the last two jokers. He had an aisle seat again. This meant that, at most, he would have only one person right next to him. Sitting in a middle seat would have been a double threat of a chance that someone who liked to chat it up would sit down next to him.

The plane's door looked as if it was about to be closed. Dan looked around and saw that the plane was less than half full with nobody sitting near him. He quietly celebrated. He started to get ready for a long winter's nap when he was interrupted by a passenger trying to get into the aisle across from him. Dan moved to the window to give the man more room to pivot into his seat. He was rather large in every way and he appeared to be sweating profusely through his wrinkled sport coat. He was wearing a striped tie which, along with the top button of his also wrinkled shirt, was loosened because it looked uncomfortable to wear. He moved to the middle seat of his row and Dan jumped for joy.

As everyone buckled up, Dan's dream of solitude started to evaporate when the big guy moved to the aisle seat. Dan was doing his best not to make eye contact with this new player. He figured that he could avoid any forthcoming chit-chat with this disheveled heap of clothes if he could keep diverting his eyes or even close them. He quietly shifted to the window seat and then closed his eyes. A few minutes went by and he thought he was in the clear until he heard a sibilant psst in his left ear. He froze. He tried pretending to be already asleep, but it was of no use. The hissing noise kept getting louder and louder until Dan finally caved and opened his eyes.

He turned to the man and asked, "Do you need something?"

The man asked, "Can I have the magazine that is sticking out of the seat pocket in front of you?

Dan responded, "Every back of the seat has one."

The man was insistent. He shook his head and said, "There isn't one in my entire row."

Dan relented and gave it to him, but he knew that this was just a ploy to start up a conversation.

In no time, Dan had once again fallen victim to a chatterbox's trap.

The man introduced himself, "Hello. I'm Andy Warwick from Muncie, Indiana."

Dan rebounded with, "Dan Becket. New York City."

Andy continued, "I'm an electrical supply company rep. I'm on my way to Finland and then the rest of northern Europe to try to gain a foothold in the markets there."

From the moment he started talking, there was no stopping him. He went from one topic to another without pausing. Dan was able to find a small break in the action and excused himself to the restroom. He washed his face over and over again as if he was trying to wash Andy's nonstop words from his skin. He dried himself and looked in the mirror. He tried to garner the courage to go back to his seat, back to the incessant useless chatter of one Andy Warwick.

He didn't think he was in there that long until he pulled the door open and saw a line of three people staring back at him. He excused himself and made it back to his seat. When he sat down, Andy went right back at it. This time, however, he asked Dan a few harmless questions about himself. Dan gave him a few generic responses.

While this was happening, weird thoughts were going through Dan's mind. He started to think back to Ted. He felt that he had been had. He figured that Ted and Trent must have had their reasons for covering up their backgrounds, but he didn't like to be on the receiving end of it. He wondered why Ted had bothered to initiate a conversation with him if he was going to lie about some of the details. Now he was wondering if Andy had any secrets of his own.

Dan looked over at the large man sweating and spitting as he rambled on about nothing. Dan concluded that he was harmless. He was, after all, built like former SNL member Chris Farley and he sweated like, well, Chris Farley. He had all of the couth of a drunk at a funeral. He was not exactly spy or assassin material. Besides, why would anyone be trailing a reporter going to do a fluff piece in Finland? Dan wasn't even certain what his assignment was. Dan's thoughts fizzled when Andy suddenly got up and headed for the restroom.

While he was alone, Dan figured that there would be no harm in doing a little investigative work on Andy. He couldn't help himself. It could be interesting. He looked over at Andy's row and his spider sense started tingling. Andy had left his overcoat on the window seat and sticking out from beneath it was at least two copies of the same magazine that he had borrowed. This was strange. Was this guy truly a spy or simply a lonely socially awkward salesman?

Dan thought for a moment and decided to ask Andy a few electrical questions when he came back. If he knew the answers, then he was probably legit. Either that or he really was a spy who took an electrical course in spy school in order to secure his cover. The questions had to be slightly technical, but not too overboard. Dan didn't want Andy to suspect that he was testing him. Dan didn't know a lot on the subject, but he had nosed around Grandma Rina's aeronautics company when he was on summer vacation as a schoolboy. She would bring him along when she could and allow him to get a first-hand education on the ins and outs of airplane building. Even though he did none of the work himself, Rina's workers took him in as an unofficial mascot and let him look over their shoulders while they were plying their trades. He got to witness plumbers, welders and electricians complete their tasks as long as he wasn't a nuisance.

Andy returned and Dan decided to get down to the business at hand. He asked, "Hey Andy, I don't know a lot about electricity, but I would like to save some money and do some DIY work at home. Can I ask for some free advice?"

Andy replied, "Certainly! What do you got?"

Dan asked, "What kind of GFCI outlets should I get if I'm gonna install a kitchen in my basement?" Dan already knew the answer. Andy responded with the right answer. Andy one and me zero, Dan thought. He went at it again, but he couldn't appear to be too anxious. "Andy, what kind of generator do you recommend I get if I want to have my entire house powered during a power outage?"

Andy replied, "Instead of doing that, you should investigate the possibility of installing a portable generator and a transfer switch. It's less intrusive on your property and costs about a fourth of the other generator installed."

Andy kept replying correctly to Dan's electrical inquiries. Not wanting to bring suspicion upon himself, Dan thought that it would be a good idea to back off. Then it happened. It was quite accidental, but it still happened. Andy slipped up and Dan was all over it.

Dan had thanked him by saying, "Thanks for the help Andy, you did Bob Vila proud."

Andy said, "Who?"

This threw Dan, so he repeated what he had said. Andy's face was blank. He had no clue as to who Bob Vila was. Andy was reasonably young, but still old enough to know the Bob Vila name. Andy was at least in his forties and anyone that age and older in the plumbing, carpentry or electrical business knew about the king of do-it-yourself home repair from TV.

Dan, recognizing what had happened, decided to go in deeper. He said to Andy, "You know, the co-star of the old TV show *Home Improvement?*"

Andy paused before saying, "Yeah, I know. I was just kidding you."

Dan's head was pulsating. Vila was the original host of *This Old House*, not the sitcom *Home Improvement*. Who is this guy? What does he want? What is so important about me that I'm being lied to again?

He sat there not even realizing whether Andy was talking or not. Maybe Andy was actually another reporter trying to steal his would-be story? Pete Sironen was already in Finland snooping around or something, but the story seemed to be taking on a life of its own. No. Andy was something other than a reporter. It seemed crazy and way overboard for a reporter to create a cover to misrepresent himself to another reporter. Dan, as devious as he could be sometimes, had never done that while on the job. He didn't know anyone who had ever done that. He would lie in order to gain access to people and places he needed for a story, but never to another reporter.

Now, he started questioning the importance of his trip. What he thought was a punishment assignment from his boss, was turning into something secretive enough to warrant having a suspicious guy on the plane. Before he started to go out of his mind with all of these crazy notions, he began to reel himself in calmly. He didn't want to lose the edge that he might have.

He sat back and closed his eyes. Even though he was too unnerved to sleep, he turned towards the window and pretended to try to get some rest. Andy looked over at him and saw that he had zoned out, so he turned to look towards his own window. Dan took a few calming breaths and realized that he just might be able to catnap. As he started to drift off, he thought back to the two hours spent listening to Andy or whoever he might really be. He couldn't believe that he was able to get him to blow his cover, at least he was fairly certain that he had.

6

IT'S NOT THE NORTH POLE,

BUT IT'S CLOSE

Dan awoke as everyone in the plane was preparing to land. He was in disbelief that he had slept. He thought he had uncovered some kind of plot against him and yet it didn't deter his need for sleep. He finally reasoned that Andy was a reporter who didn't follow the normal protocol when trying to beat out a fellow reporter for a scoop. This had a soothing effect on him and allowed him to relax. He opened his eyes, leaned over to look out the window and saw it. Finland. What a beautiful place, even in the dark. Snow covered everything. He was used to snow, but it still looked unbelievable shimmering under the moonlit and city-lit sky. He could only say, "Amazing."

He had been to a lot of places in the world. This should have felt routine to him, but it didn't. It had a different vibe attached to it. He didn't want to think the word magical in his thoughts for fear that it might seem too sickeningly-sweet. He couldn't explain the feeling even to himself. He didn't remember the last time he felt this way about a place that he hadn't stepped foot on yet. He didn't think there was ever a first time. He was always irritable about traveling outside the United States. It was usually when he had to visit his parents. He did, however, always enjoy visiting his grandparents when they were in Europe, especially Rina.

The plane touched down on the runway at Helsinki-Vantaa International Airport. Helsinki looked amazing from the air. He was ready to get started, but he still had a long way to go. He would be in Helsinki for about three more hours before boarding another plane for Rovaniemi.

He had never been to this part of Europe before. The closest he had come was Germany from visiting with his parents on one of their many business trips. He had also done an overnight in Denmark along its border with Germany. Cold weather was not on his list of favorite things, even though he had gone on many ski trips while in college. He was quite good at skiing, but he was not a loyal fan of cold snowy weather. He had learned the sport and went on numerous excursions with his buddies as a way to meet girls.

New York City had the weather he liked, not too cold and not too hot. Finland was never on his radar of places to visit during the winter. However, at this moment, he was fascinated. He also hadn't stepped outside yet. That would come after he deplaned in Rovaniemi. He had been to the Alps several times and was familiar with this type of cold. Familiar yes, but used to it, no. Because of Finland's arctic circle proximity, wintertime temperatures generally remain below zero degrees centigrade. Finland's combination of geographic and meteorological characteristics was the perfect recipe for both adventure and disaster for Dan; his temperate climate upbringing has not prepared him for this latest stint as an investigative reporter and his occasional acidic personality does not generally prepare him to work as a member of a team, although he never needs to be questioned about his feelings of loyalty, he just has to show his friends and acquaintances more.

Now as Dan gathered his things, he looked over at Andy and noticed that he looked very frazzled. Andy turned towards him and said, "I've never gotten used to flying. I hate the take-offs and the landings and everything in between. That's why I talk so much when we're in flight."

Dan was amused by this. He was believing more and more that Andy was not a major threat. He was interested, though, to see if Andy would be on the next flight with him. If he was, then Dan would continue to be suspicious. If he wasn't, then Dan would be relieved.

Grabbing everything he had with him, Dan headed down the aisle and out the door. He slowed down to wait for Andy to say goodbye. Andy finally caught up to him after clumsily getting his bag and trying to get his big frame out of the plane. They walked quietly for a short time. Andy didn't feel the need to talk anymore because he was comfortably on terra firma. Dan was heading to get something to eat while waiting for his next flight and he asked Andy, "Do you want to join me for dinner?"

Andy politely declined. He said, "I'm going into the city to meet with representatives from a few Finnish supply companies."

He reached to shake Dan's hand and said, "Have a safe trip."

Dan shook Andy's clammy hand and wished him the same. They both turned from each other and walked away. Dan glanced back briefly and watched Andy head towards the baggage area. Andy wasn't going to Rovaniemi. Dan laughed to himself about all of his elaborate delusions about this average joe from Indiana. He went and got some food.

The rest of his plane excursion was uneventful. He didn't try to sleep on his flight to Rovaniemi. It was like tempting fate. He figured trying to nap would only invite someone to talk to him. It happened with Ted. It happened with Andy. The flight was mostly full and Dan had people all around him this time. Nobody spoke to him. There were a few polite pardon me's and conversations going on in Finnish with Swedish mixed in for good measure. He put his air pods in and shuffled some vintage rock music. His eyebrows raised when he heard his first song, ELO's *Strange Magic.* He thought of Ted and grinned.

After the plane touched down, a flight attendant got on the intercom and announced the greeting. "Welcome to Rovaniemi, the capital city of Lapland, Finland and the official hometown of Santa Claus!" Dan was not familiar with the yule designation given to this obvious hub of holiday festivities. He picked up his luggage at the baggage claim and called Pete Sironen about a ride.

Pete and his cousin Jaako were about twenty-five minutes away, so Dan decided to investigate Rovaniemi on his laptop. He looked at the itinerary sheet that Hildie from the newspaper had given him. He looked up Rovaniemi and found it to have exploded with the Christmas spirit. The area in and around this city of now over sixty-three thousand people had embraced the idea of being the home of Santa Claus or Joulupukki, as he was called in Finland. This was thanks to a Finnish radio announcer named Markus Rautio who, back in 1927, had declared on his radio program that Joulupukki lived in Finland. He pinpointed that this particular Santa-like person lived hours north and east on Korvatunturi Mountain.

Dan learned that Korvatunturi, which literally means 'ear fell' in Finnish, is located inside Urho Kekkonen National Park. A fell is a term most closely associated with parts of Scandinavia and the United Kingdom. Its location put it right on the Russian border. According to legend, this highland area with its ear shape helped Santa listen in on people, specifically children, to find out if they had been good all year. His Finnish name Joulupukki once meant Yule Goat. The goat idea was borrowed from the Nordic tales of Thor and his goat-pulled chariot.

In early tales, the Yule Goat Joulupukki was actually a menacing spirit or demon who terrorized young children. His mighty horns conjured up scary images that kept young people awake at night. Later, much softer stories had him using powers of invisibility to spy on townspeople to make sure that the rites of Christmas were being observed. Eventually, the idea of him being part animal in nature seemed to just fade away. His helpers were called the Tonttu or little people. They were not the stereotypical elves. They were suspicious, unfriendly and sometimes even dangerous, if crossed. About the only thing similar between America's image of St. Nick and Finland's was that reindeer were used to pull his sleigh, even though Joulupukki's pullers couldn't fly. Ironically, Coca-Cola's rendition of Santa was created by a descendant of Finnish immigrants.

Dan continued his search with more items from his piece of paper. Savukoski was his eventual destination. By searching *Wikipedia,* he found that even though Savukoski was a very small town, it encompassed a large number of square kilometers. It was on the fringe of the land of fables that he had just been reading about. Living in Savukoski might mean that your next-door neighbor could be an hour away. Dan's phone buzzed indicating Pete's arrival. He packed up his bags and walked out the door to the coldness of Lapland. Pete and Jaako were in a well-maintained 2007 Toyota SUV. Pete was outside of it with the back door opened and he reached out and grabbed Dan's biggest suitcase. He then put it inside. He gently tossed the others in too, shook Dan's hand and then both men jumped into the vehicle.

Dan was in the back seat and Pete said, "This is my cousin Jake." He grinned at Jaako when Americanizing his name.

Dan responded to the driver, "Pleased to meet you, Jake."

Jaako let the bastardization of his name go unchallenged and promptly put the SUV in gear and pulled off of the curb while Pete asked, "How was your flight?"

Dan replied, "I met some unique characters along the way, to say the least."

Pete commented, "Speaking of characters, wait until you meet the rest of my family." Jaako looked over at the two of them and smirked. A few moments went by and then Dan took a deep but quiet breath.

Dan wasted no more time and fired off with, "So what's going on here? Why was I sent all this way? What's the big spooky secret?" Pete looked over at Jaako and then turned to Dan. Dan looked at Jaako and said, "Sorry. Can we speak in front of your cousin?"

Pete and Jaako both quickly responded, "Of course." Pete slapped his trying-to-be funny cousin on the shoulder and said, "My cousins are the ones who let me in on all of this. I let Roger know about a series of very strange events that happened right before I got here. My cousins and some of their friends gave details of stories from people they know who live near the Russian border. It seems that they witnessed movement by Russian personnel along the two countries' boundary line. They're not sure if it was the military because no weapons were openly displayed. They did see what appeared to be surveillance and/or monitoring equipment pointed at Korvatunturi Fell, which is a very special mountain to many Finns, if not downright sacred to some. The people living in the surrounding areas of the national park near this highland are few in number, but they take exception to any disruption to their daily lives. Lives which have remained virtually unchanged for centuries, in many aspects."

As Pete was about to explain the historical importance of the region, Dan interrupted him to save him from having to give a long oration. "I know the holiday importance of the fell. I read about it online. I also know that some of the legend goes all the way back to Nordic mythology and the days of Thor."

Pete was impressed. He had heard stories about Dan's personality. He knew he was a go-getter, but he also knew from previously working with him that Dan could be a tough nut to crack. He had first-hand experience witnessing Dan's behavior when he wasn't happy about an assignment he drew. He could be indignant and indifferent, but in the end, he always accomplished the end goal.

Dan continued with, "What I want to know is about the supernatural aura tag that Roger had placed on all of this. What's this all about?"

Pete began his story telling again. "Strange sounds seem to come from this mountain. They weren't extremely loud, at least not to the surrounding villages. But to the people in the tiny hamlets and settlements near the fell, they were loud enough, with ground shaking movements to go along with them."

Dan interrupted again. "Earthquakes. Earthquakes are not supernatural." He shifted back in his seat.

Pete looked out the window and with a cool demeanor replied, "Earthquakes would be the answer if it was the only phenomenon here, but there's something else."

Dan asked, "Something else?"

Pete nodded. "At the same time of the sounds and quaking, there was a strange glow briefly emanating from the fell. A glow that has never been seen before by anyone currently alive."

Dan asked, "What do you mean by anyone alive?"

Pete went on with his depiction of historical events. "According to folklore, a glow was seen in this area more than a century ago. And before that, hundreds of years more, and before that, etcetera, etcetera."

Dan stared out his window and said, "Volcanic activity. That's the only explanation." He looked at Pete.

Pete stared back at him and calmly responded. "That would make perfect sense if not for the fact that the glow doesn't stay on. I read up on volcanic activity and plate tectonics. This doesn't add up to that." There was a pause in the verbal tennis game going on between the two reporters. The pause was brief but deafeningly quiet until Pete took a shallow breath and said, "And then there's the dead bodies."

7

THE TIMES, THEY REALLY ARE A-CHANGIN'

Dan looked blankly at Pete. "Bodies?"

Pete looked over at Jaako and gave him a nod to speak. "Yes." Jaako replied. "Distant relatives of ours who live near the fell found charred remains of at least one human-like creature. It scared them enough to travel hours to see my brothers and me with only this bit of partial evidence." He handed Dan an object that was obscured by cloth it was wrapped in.

Dan unwrapped the cloth and pulled out what appeared to be about a six-inch blade of some sort. It was unlike any blade Dan had ever seen. The blade was dark in color. He couldn't tell whether it was naturally colored that way or had been burned in a fire. The handle was almost non-existent. It had apparently been torched to almost nothing.

Jaako continued with his description. "The bodies were so badly burned that we couldn't tell if they were human or animal or whatever." He looked at Dan through the rearview mirror before speaking again. "We believe that there were a total of four bodies."

"Believe?" Dan asked.

"Yes. Believe. It was as if they were welded together."

With confusion written all over his face, Dan asked, "Why didn't anyone call the police? Why did they come to you? Pete, why am I here? What could I possibly do that could be of more help than the authorities?"

Pete waited for the barrage of questions to end before he offered up this explanation. "Look Dan, the people living in this area have an extreme sense of independence. They don't want the local or federal authorities involved for fear that they may get more involved in their day to day lives. Sure, they want it solved, but these individuals are used to being left alone by the law. Most of them don't even live in a town. They're more like small settlements and in many cases, they live far away from even another house."

Dan didn't get the answers he wanted. He asked, "But what is my purpose here?"

"I wanted you here Dan," Pete answered quickly.

Dan looked completely lost and asked, "Why? What is it that you're not telling me?"

Pete and Jaako exchanged glances until Jaako summoned the courage to explain. "It's not just the settlers in this region that don't want the government around. We don't want them either. The family members that we spoke of that live near the Korvatunturi Fell are actually our grandparents, Pete's and mine. Our sister Kirsti, another of Pete's cousins, lives with them. We believe that there would be some form of a government cover-up that would simply relocate the people rather than deal with this very strange situation. We figured that if there is no real earth-shattering story here, then nobody need know and there would be no harm, no foul. Your boss would be mad and I know this sounds selfish, but that doesn't concern us. However, if there truly is a major story at hand, strange or not, then you could get the story out there. That would afford our family and other people we know, some security from being displaced. They would have to do an actual public investigation. Publicity is not what any government wants."

Dan was still in the dark. "How can the government forcibly move people whose homesteads have been there for many generations?"

Jaako replied, "The government can only do it to the people who live in the national park. The homes that were there before the park was established and stayed in the same family were allowed to remain under an agreement with Helsinki. However, if the safety of the people is threatened for any reason, the agreement stipulates that they can be removed from the park and then relocated."

Pete interceded, "Jaako is a park ranger, so he's similar to a police officer. He knows how this all works."

Dan paused and then asked, "Why would there be a need for a cover-up? You have a dead body. You investigate. Case closed."

Jaako responded first. "It's not that simple. The people living there are not going to be very cooperative. There will be push back on this, if I'm saying that right. Even though our police forces throughout the country have an approval rating of well over ninety percent, these settlements have enjoyed so much independence for generations. They will not respond well to an investigation and our police will do everything in their power to solve this."

Dan still didn't get it. "I'm lost. I'm truly lost. So why would there be a cover-up? The investigation will obviously be a very transparent and overt operation. Your country's population will pay attention. Any attempt by your government to remove them would make it into your newspapers. You don't need me for that." Dan looked at them both. "Come on. Tell me what you're not telling me."

There was endless silence that only actually lasted about ten seconds until Pete spoke. "The government will definitely try to conceal as much as it can. All governments would, the U.S., Britain, Russia, China and pretty much everywhere else." Pete hesitated again before continuing. "There were several dead bodies and they didn't look human."

Dan asked him, "Why would dead animals launch such a big investigation and then a cover-up? What were they, reindeer, bears or whatever kinds of animal's you guys have here?"

Jaako stepped in with his own answer. "None of the above. We can't tell. Anyone who has seen them can't tell. Some seem to have horns, but don't look like anything we've seen. Some look like dogs, but not the kind you have around the house or even pull a sled with. They're huge, I mean really huge."

Dan's face was a combination of disbelief and disgust. He responded back, "Really? You're talking fairytale stuff. This is totally ridiculous."

Pete added another beauty to the mix. "And one of the bodies is an animal and it isn't. It's human and it isn't. It looks like a person, but its size and dimensions are all off. All of these carcasses are so badly torched that nobody can tell what they are."

All three men took a breather for a few moments before Pete brought up another reason for Dan to investigate without police involvement. "Right now, you and I are the only journalists who know about this. The police don't know. Nobody outside of this part of the park knows. Roger Harbinger wants to keep it that way. Whatever Roger told you back in New York was probably a lie. He just wanted to get you here without any trouble from you. And do you know why?"

Dan gave him the obvious, "Why?"

Pete answered him. "Because the *New York Times* wants to buy our newspaper. All of it. Roger would be brought over, you and me probably, and just about everybody else in the newsroom. Roger wants this more than anything. The owners want it. Roger figures that if we or mainly you come through, then it's a done deal and he will be rewarded with a promotion and a much bigger paycheck. The icing on the cake would be that the story gets out to the public before any other newspapers find out, even Finland's. If Roger doesn't get a story from you, then that's on him. After all, he's the one who forced this assignment on you."

Dan took all of this in for a couple of minutes before Pete commented again. "Think of this. If all of this carnage is explainable, then no worries. The police will have to be notified, but they will likely not feel that the lives of the settlers are in danger enough to warrant them being removed. If there is a bigger eerie story here and we find it, we will get it out before anyone." Dan mulled over what was just said and then Pete added more. "The best thing is that we can move about freely without interference because nobody has got a clue."

Dan cut into Pete's speech. "Does the U.S. government know? You know, I mean does the White House know?" Pete shook his head no and said, "I doubt it. We're alone in this."

Dan looked out the window before quietly responding, "Yeah, we're alone all right. It's just us…and the Russians."

8

LITTLE VALLEY

Dan watched the scenery go by in the dark as the car continued towards its eventual destination of Savukoski, which meant he got to see very little. They stopped once to get something to eat in Sodankyla and then moved along to Savukoski. None of them spoke of the original conversation the rest of the way, but everyone knew it was still on each other's minds. They talked about the way of life in this part of Lapland and Dan asked some questions about the Sironen family. He didn't want to make it seem like he was digging for information, but that's exactly what he was doing. He tried to avoid asking too many questions because he suspected that Pete would figure it out rather easily. Which he did.

Pete didn't mind that Dan was doing his job by inquiring about the family. Jaako didn't seem to notice and the rest of the trip was basically uneventful. They arrived in Savukoski, the supposed final stop of Dan's long journey. This proved to be less than accurate. To say that the Sironen family cabin was in Savukoski was a misstatement. The cabin was still many rugged miles north and east of this small town. Savukoski was the postal designation of the cabin and the final piece of organized civilization, but that was as close as the two places were in relation to each other.

The cabin was located in an area known to the locals as Pieni Laakso or Little Valley in English. Its location put it close to a village called Tulppio. There were no permanent year-round residents in Tulppio, officially, but there were houses on the outskirts like the Sironen's. The area was very close to the Russian border. Pete's family homestead was less than fifteen miles from Russia and less than twenty miles from Finland's version of *Area 51,* Korvatunturi, the object of Dan's journalistic desire. It was way past sunset when the three arrived at the temporary end of their travels. Jaako's brothers, Aleksi and Arturo, were there waiting and came outside when they heard the sound of the SUV's engine. They went right to the back of the vehicle to get Dan's bags without exchanging pleasantries because of the extreme cold. After entering the house, they put the luggage down. Pete introduced everybody and Arturo asked, "Does anyone want something to eat? Some tea, maybe? Coffee or something stronger?"

Dan settled for coffee and the men retired to the surprisingly large living room. Dan didn't get much of a chance to see the outside of the cabin when they arrived. It was too dark. Snow completely covered the roof to the point where it hung over the eaves. There was more snow that had climbed up a couple of feet on the outside walls of the cabin due to either the wind or a snowblower. The place looked ancient in style, but was well-maintained and sturdy, part stone and part wood inside and out. It was a perfect combination. The wood on the outside had been replaced here and there due to the elements, but the interior wood was almost completely original with just a few repairs done over the last fifty years.

Even though everyone was there for a very serious reason, Dan noticed that Pete and his cousins interacted with each other in a very stress-free comical sort of way. Miles and years apart failed to stop them from feeling at ease with one another. Jaako appeared to lead the way in tormenting Pete and the jokes came one right after the other. Dan thought he was watching a sitcom. He became confused when they heard the three Finns call Pete by the name Pez. Alexi explained. "The name Pez is a play on the three initials of Pete's name."

Jaako asked Dan his full name and he reluctantly said, "Daniel Evan Becket."

The three cousins shouted at the same time, "Your name is Deb!" Dan shook his head thinking that this was how it was going to be hanging around with these clowns. All he heard for the rest of the night from the brothers was, "Hey Deb! Excuse me Deb!"

Finally, Dan stood and said, "Well, tomorrow's a big day. We've got to go take a look at the fell and maybe take a quick look to see what the Russians are up to."

Jaako added, "And don't forget the dead bodies!"

Dan agreed. "Right. We've got to go and check them out too."

He looked over at Pete and asked, "Could someone direct me to my room?"

Arturo took the initiative and said, "I will. Follow me. It's this way."

Dan said, "Thanks." Then he followed him.

Pete's cousins were going to cram into the biggest bedroom, which had two beds and a large chair that could fit an average sized man. The room was actually the living room seventy years ago, until their great-grandfather and some of his friends modified it. The present living room was only half its size before the renovation took place. Most of the upstairs didn't even exist until all of this took place. The cabin was more than just a cabin now. It was a house and a good sized one at that. The long-ago Sironens would hardly recognize the old homestead.

Pete showed Dan his room. The two men exchanged some final words and then both said, "Good night." Dan unpacked only some of his clothes, knowing that he would probably be packing his things all over again in the morning. He showered and climbed into bed with thoughts of the fell, strange glows, Russians and dead bodies dancing in his head. He took one last look at his cell phone, texted Nancy and Roger that he had arrived. He didn't wait for them to respond, put his air pods in and laughed. The random song list that he requested started off playing what was starting to become his personal anthem, ELO's *Strange Magic*. He closed his eyes and was gone.

9

BORDER PATROL

Dan awoke to the sounds of the Sironens making breakfast. Pots were banging, dishes placed on the table and voices at normal volume could be heard emanating throughout the house. Dan quickly changed and fixed up his room before descending below to say his hellos.

Aleksi asked, "Coffee?"

He gladly accepted. He took a seat after offering to help with the table settings, but he was politely refused when Arturo said, "Sit. We got this. You're our guest."

After all of the preparations were made, everybody was seated and dug into the food and beverages. A few minutes after everyone was enjoying their meal, Pete began the discussion everyone knew was coming.

"So, Dan, what do you think of this? We have six snowmobiles ready to go. They're sitting in the building next to the garage. While the three of us were coming from the airport, Arturo and

Aleksi put together a survival pack for all of us including food, drink, backpacks, portable shelters and clean woolen socks. We have guns, knives, flares, snowshoes with poles and cheap night vision glasses. Everything is on the machines already, along with extra fuel."

Dan said, "I'm impressed."

It seemed that Pete and his family were well prepared. Pete proceeded to explain the plan of attack. "Sunrise in Lapland is several hours away, but there will be enough light eventually. I think leaving within the hour would be best. It will take us a couple of hours on the trails to go past the fell to see where the Russians are and to do a little spying. Then we can double back and head for the fell to sniff around a bit. After all of that, we'll finally travel to our grandparents' place and stay for at least a night or two."

Dan started to wonder about Pete. Roger Harbinger didn't seem to give him a lot of credit as a reporter. There's more to Pete than meets the eye, Dan thought. He's organized and seems like a take charge kind of guy but Dan was curious to see what else Pete had up his sleeve.

Pete omitted two items from their itinerary. He failed to mention when they would see the bodies and that they would stop at a friend's house and exchange their snowmobiles for either an electric powered SUV or a couple of dog sled teams. He planned on telling Dan about these two ditties later. As they all got up from the table, Dan realized that Pete had said that there were six machines ready to go, but there were only five of them.

He spoke up. "Pete, you said there's six machines ready. Is somebody else coming?"

As if right on cue, a knock at the door could be heard and Jaako answered it. After a few exchanges of pleasantries, Pete turned to Dan and said, "Dan this is Mikko Kurtti, a friend and distant relative who lives fairly close to the fell. He knows the layout of the land as well as Jaako, if not better."

Jaako protested from the kitchen with, "Hey!" Jaako traveled the land constantly in his job as a ranger. He probably knew the land better than the settlers that lived in that area.

The men went and got their winter gear. Pete said to Dan, "Come with me. Nothing you have will protect you enough from the conditions we will encounter." He led Dan to a closet near the door to the garage. Pete opened it and said, "Here. Take these." He provided Dan with warm headgear that would fit under the helmet that was waiting for him in the garage. He also gave Dan a snowsuit, a heavy, hooded jacket and a pair of gloves. Pete showed Dan that he was equipped with a small digital camera with a decent zoom lens. Pete wasn't officially a photographer, but he was pretty good at it.

They entered the garage and Pete manually lifted the garage door after they had dressed. The bitter cold punched Dan square in the face and he scrambled to put his face mask on and then his helmet. They walked outside to join the other men in the heated building where the snowmobiles awaited the riders.

The Sironen boys had a unique setup in this building. The snowmobiles were facing outward along the width of the building on a smooth metal floor that stretched a foot longer on each side of the two outer machines. Mikko had put his own machine in the garage because it was very old and he had ridden over an hour on it without stopping. Eventually, Aleksi pressed a button on a remote after everyone had fired up their engines and the metal floor tilted towards the outside, giving the machines a little boost when exiting.

Mikko and Jaako took the lead and left first. They were followed by Pete, Dan, Aleksi and Arturo. Aleksi and Arturo stopped and Aleksi pressed the remote again and the floor tilted back level again. One more press of the remote and the doors closed. The last two riders pulled on their throttles and then stopped a hundred feet later, where the rest of the group was waiting. Aleksi threw the remote to Jaako and he promptly put it in an insulated box attached to a tree on the side of the road. Then they were off again in three sets of two for the next several miles until they took a detour to a trail that only allowed them to travel in a single file.

Along the way, Dan had a good laugh to himself. No one had even asked him if he could ride one of these machines. The Finns, including Pete, took it for granted. This activity was automatic for the five, given their upbringing. But for Dan, not so much. He had spent a great deal of time, when he could, near water. He loved the ocean and large lakes. He loved to waterski, handle the tiller of a sailboat and even occasionally surf when time allowed. He also had ample experience with jet skis.

The times he spent with his parents in the Alps provided him with some experience on these vehicles, but he was easily the most novice rider of the crew. Dan had already guessed that Mikko and Pete's cousins were ex-military or ex-law enforcement, given how methodical they all were in executing this mission. He started thinking that Pete might be too. This made Dan the weak link in the chain. He definitely felt that way.

After an hour straight in the saddle, the men pulled to the side of the trail to go on another even smaller path. A few minutes later they came upon a small group of buildings with two small cabins, a tool shed and a building that appeared to be used as a garage. Mikko led the way to the garage, dismounted and swung open the twin doors. He motioned to the men to follow suit. They obliged and he brought out some gas containers and they refueled. The sun was partially up, but the sky was overcast and the frigid temperatures bit at any exposed body parts.

When the six had completed their task, Mikko motioned to follow him into one of the cabins.

They entered a short hallway where they took off their helmets, face masks, gloves and heavy coats. Mikko said, "Come on in and we'll get some hot tea and warm up for a few minutes." He opened the door to the rest of the cabin and they followed closely behind. The room they entered had a fireplace going at full roar. Mugs were at the table already, with covered baskets of Karelian pies and a large bowl of porridge.

Mikko's wife Katriina came into the room and greeted them with a welcoming smile. She quickly said, "Please, sit down, get warm and have some hot coffee and biscuits." The men graciously sat down and each politely reached for the food as Katriina brought the coffee pot around to each man. Porridge was familiar to Dan, but not the pies. These little delicacies had a rye crust with a rice porridge filling. Dan bit in and instantly fell in love.

Time was of the essence, so the men ate quickly and cleaned up after themselves even though Katriina insisted that they leave everything there. While they were putting all of their outer garments back on, Mikko's sleeping children awoke and came out to hug their father. They were very young. Dan guessed that they were no more than six or seven.

Mikko announced, "Ahhhh, here are my pikku lapsi, Anja and Erno!" Anja was a platinum blonde little girl with very blue eyes. Erno was a good-sized lad with a mop of dirty blonde hair. Both children wrapped themselves around their dad to say goodbye. They also hugged their three Finn cousins and politely went over to Pete whom they had only met twice before. Mikko had the children go over and shake Dan's hand, which they did without argument.

They went quickly to their machines and waited for Mikko, who came out with walkie talkie headsets for three. He said, "Here. One for every two people. That's all I have." Dan was paired off with Jaako. They would stay in the rear. If they were to unfortunately get separated from the others, Jaako knew the terrain. Pete and Aleksi were put in as the middle twosome. Pete hadn't been in this area since he was a young man and was not too familiar with the area around the fell. Aleksi was an avid hunter, hiker and all-around outdoorsman. If they were to get separated from the rest, Aleksi could easily guide them to safety. At the front would be Mikko and Arturo. Mikko was the most familiar with the geography of the land, despite Jaako's earlier protest. Arturo was an avid outdoorsman like his brother Aleksi, but he wasn't as familiar with the fell like his siblings. It made sense for him to be paired with Mikko.

Each person's helmet contained a very short-range radio system that would extend about two miles. They could all communicate with each other as long as they stayed within reasonable proximity. The three walkie talkies had a range of approximately thirty-eight miles, which could also communicate with Mikko's wife Katriina. Mikko had a short-wave radio set up at his residence and Katriina had instructions to keep it on in case there was an emergency. The group could also keep in contact with many residents both in Finland and Russia. Settlers relied on these radios because cell phones were not usable in most parts of this region.

The six were on their way towards Russia, but Dan started thinking about the dead bodies. He spoke on his helmet radio, "When are we going to see the remains that were found?" There was silence for a moment. Mikko and Pete were waiting to see who would answer him first.

Pete responded first. "We're going to the Russian border first. On the trip back, we will head towards the fell where we can show you the bodies."

The group traversed the snow laden countryside on little used hiking paths for as long as they could. The trek was nearly impossible. The paths provided some solid ground, but several times the group had to stop because one or more of the machines had sunk in the deep snow or had hit an unseen obstacle that was buried. It was also somewhat dark even though it was the middle of the day. After two hours, they turned and went down a small embankment. Minutes later, they came upon another cabin with a decent sized shed.

The two buildings were totally swamped with snow. The place would have looked like it was abandoned had it not been for the recently shoveled front and back door to the tiny cabin. The area around the shed had also been cleared. Everything else seemed to have been purposely left to make the homestead look quite uninhabitable. Mikko led the men to the shed where he opened the doors and showed them their next mode of transportation. "This is our next ride."

The SUV was completely white, including the windows; nothing was shiny. Anything that could reflect had been removed. Its body was covered with a material that was different from normal passenger vehicles. Mikko said that it was made of a dielectric composite. Dan and Pete had no idea what Mikko was talking about until he said that the material rendered the automobile virtually undetectable by radar.

One important item that Mikko added was that they could still be spotted by a plane, helicopter or astonishingly by a satellite. He went up to one of the doors and called the rest of them over in order to show them something. Removing his gloves, he peeled off the white tint from the window and instructed the men to do the same with all of the windows. He said that because they were traveling in limited daylight, the all-white vehicle might stick out against the eventual dark countryside. After all of the windows were done, he opened the rear door and placed the tinting material in the back and brought out black colored versions. The six got to work without speaking and placed the black material on all of the windows.

Mikko walked around to make sure that everything looked satisfactory before showing them their next task. He went to the same door that he had started with and tugged hard and pulled off one of the white panels. Turning it around, he showed the others that its flip side was black. He snapped the panel in and told the others to be careful not to damage anything. They had to place all of the panel pieces in carefully and securely as if they were doing a jigsaw puzzle. If any one piece was not properly placed, the result could mean the loss of a panel or two in either high winds or the normal jostling of the vehicle over the rough trails. It took a while, but the men accomplished their goal.

Mikko said, "Take everything from your snowmobiles, except for your helmets, and put all belongings in the back. Bring all of the weapons to where you'll be sitting."

He grabbed a somewhat large bag that was in the shed and threw it on top of all of the supplies. With all of this preparation going on, Dan knew that Mikko was not just your run-of-the-mill family friend. He had to be involved with the government or the military, or at the very least, was once involved.

Mikko then got in the driver's seat, closed the door and fired up the engine. The engine made no sound. He pulled the SUV out of the shed and stopped. Getting out, he said that it was electric. A gas or diesel engine would not only make a great deal of noise, but it could be detected if anyone was using listening devices. He had all of them bring their machines into the shed and then he closed the doors. Before everyone took their seats, he opened the rear door and took out the bag that he had placed in the back earlier. Opening it, he took out white ski masks and tossed one to each man. "Here, put these on later when we exit the auto." He also took out very thin white coverings and had each one put one on over their snowsuits, telling them to be very careful because they could tear easily.

"If we are on schedule, there should be enough daylight so that we will need to blend in with the surrounding snow. If we arrive at our destination late, then we'll go back to our dark coverings."

Mikko instructed everyone to jump in the SUV. It was a very tight fit with three in the front and three in the back. Each man was of at least normal size, but with all of the winter gear on them, it was like squeezing in six sumo wrestlers. As Mikko pulled the automobile away from the residence, Dan asked, "Are we going to let the people inside the residence know that we've been here?"

Mikko said, "They already know. But no. They're either not home or they don't want us to go in anyway."

Dan looked confused. Pete turned to Dan and whispered, "Smugglers. They don't want outsiders like you and me to see them. And they're close friends of Mikko's."

Dan looked at Pete for a moment and then turned to look out the window. He started thinking that maybe Pete was more heavily involved with all of this than he had let on.

After a few minutes, Dan asked Mikko, "If we're wearing white to blend in with the snow, then why did we go dark with the SUV's color? Won't people see us coming miles away?" Dan had thought that he made a good point.

Mikko said, "That makes sense, but I'm more worried about getting back undercover. We will be traveling on a route that has a lot of trees. We should be fine most of the way. However, when we travel outside the vehicle and attempt to spy on the Russians, we will be partially exposed. White clothing will be better. It should be dark most of the trip back."

The SUV rode fairly smoothly and was quiet due to a lack of a combustible engine. The downside was that it didn't have great range. The vehicle had been converted to electric about three years earlier and the batteries had been charged over and over again. Mikko had said that the auto could go nearly two hundred miles on a highway before having to recharge. Because they moved very slowly across rough terrain and had a great deal of weight inside, he estimated that it was probably good for about one-fifty. He tried to re-assure everybody by saying, "We should have no issues about getting back before losing power. Total round trip should be roughly forty to fifty miles, provided we have no problems."

Despite the bumpy and almost impossible trail, the vehicle lumbered on for about three miles until they came to a fairly wide and very smooth surface. The vehicle slid slightly when Mikko drove and he said, "This is actually a very shallow stream. If we should fall through, we can keep going without any trouble. The rest of the trip to the Russian border should be fairly uneventful except for an occasional skid here and there."

The SUV had studded tires, which were able to grip the ice covering the stream bed with relative ease, but Mikko was careful. The rest of their excursion to the border was reasonably quick and painless. The last three miles were the most difficult because the group had to turn off of the stream bed and continue on an almost never-traveled trail. They continued on successfully, but very slowly.

Mikko suddenly stopped the vehicle and said, "This is the end of the road for us. We have to hike the rest of the way for about a mile." Everybody removed themselves from their seats and climbed out onto a crusty snow surface. Dan was quietly complaining in his mind, but then he realized that even though the ground was slippery, it was firm. He hated the cold, but after he put his white ski mask and gloves on, he felt much better. They were lucky. The sun was still just below the horizon and there was no appreciable wind blowing at them.

They unloaded most of the gear from the back, including the snowshoes and poles. Everyone grabbed a rifle with ammunition, a knife and a flare. Mikko, Aleksi and Jaako also took a pistol and the long-distance walkie talkies. They left the survival supplies such as food, sleeping bags and tents. With Mikko and Jaako now leading, they departed as soon as everyone had put on their snowshoes.

Dan was in good shape, but he found this type of travel extremely difficult. He kept up with the other men, but it was not pleasurable. The only member of their little secret society to outwardly show fatigue in his body language was Pete. He was still a young man of thirty, but he was not used to the rigors of this type of activity. His cousins, of course, saw what he was going through and tortured him for it. They were used to this type of winter activity, having lived in this environment all of their lives.

Mikko, who at forty-five, was clearly the oldest of the group. He sped along seamlessly, despite his relatively huge body size. He was ruggedly built and easily much bigger than the rest. He looked as if he could pick up a person by their face. He had a long curly graying beard and the look of someone who should be asking children what they wanted for Christmas.

After nearly a full mile of this frozen hell, Mikko motioned for everyone to get down. He stabbed his poles into the ground, removed his snowshoes and encouraged his companions to do the same. While they were following his lead, he began to crawl on his stomach to the top of a small ridge. The snow was soft and powdery. He amazed them with his spryness. When Mikko got to the top, he stopped and took out a pair of binoculars that he had beneath his jacket. While the rest of the men made their way to him, he looked towards the Russian border. They were only a few hundred yards away from Russia in the area where the Russians had been spotted monitoring something in the direction of Korvatunturi.

When everyone caught up to him, they were surprised when he suddenly moved to his knees. He waved for everyone to do the same. Mikko pointed and said, "They're gone! They packed up and left!" He then proceeded to say a few words in Finnish, probably curse words, Dan guessed. After each person took a turn with the binoculars, they stood up and started walking carefully towards the border. They were currently at an elevation that was higher than the area that had their attention.

The men finally made it to about a hundred yards away, when Mikko yelled, "Get down!" The six hit the ground and kept their heads down as Mikko loudly whispered, "Border patrol. They're on snowmobiles." Mikko slowly lifted his head and the other five did the same. The patrol consisted of three machines, each with an armed soldier.

Mikko shocked the others when he took out his rifle and pointed it in the direction of the patrol. He had the look of a sniper about to pick off his prey, but he was only looking through the rifle's scope to get a more precise view. The rest hesitated, but eventually copied his actions, except for Pete. He had taken out his camera and was already snapping away with the zoom lens attached. They could see that the soldiers were careful to hug the boundary between the two countries.

In an instant everything changed. Without warning or a sound to alert them, Arturo fell back in pain. The youngest of them had been hit by something. Before anyone could move, the snowy powder was alive with bullets landing all around them. No gunshots could be heard, which made it even more confusing. They were paralyzed with fear and the inability to move even an inch. Even though they were dressed in snow-colored clothing, the men appeared to be easy marks.

Jaako moved first by rolling down the slight incline to a spot that seemed to provide some cover. Then it was Aleksi, Pete, Dan and Mikko. Jaako crawled over to his wounded brother and pulled him even further away. He looked Arturo up and down and found that he had been shot not once, but twice. He had been grazed on the right side of his neck and the left side of his head. The barrage stopped, but the six of them were still unwilling to move.

Aleksi, in a low but firm voice, warned, "We have to get out of here now. It's insane to think that they won't finish the job."

Arturo, despite his wounds, was making light of the situation. "I haven't had this much action since *Nam*." Dan looked confused, but Pete and Mikko were quite familiar with the three brothers' sense of humor.

Pete looked over at a befuddled Dan and said, "Don't mind him, he's got a weird sense of what's funny. He's watched too many American movies. But he was in Iraq though."

Dan and Pete were the only ones who had no military experience, but none of the six had expected anything like this. Jaako and Aleksi pulled Arturo out of the line of fire by sliding down the slight mound of snow. The other three slid on their own and all of them reached for a pair of snowshoes. After getting them on, they each took a set of poles and awkwardly trudged along the path they had just created. Mikko kept shouting at them to move quickly. About two hundred yards later, Mikko motioned for them to stop.

He said, "Let's take a look at Arturo's wounds. Jaako, Aleksi, Dan, you guys spread out and keep watch. Pete and I will take a look at Arturo." Dan moved with the other two and found some cover. He did have experience firing a weapon, but he wondered why none of the Finns had asked him if he did. Perhaps they just assumed that, because he was American, he knew all about guns. He looked out to where they had just come from and pointed his rifle in that direction. Wild thoughts were in his head. What has he gotten himself into now? He's been in regions around the world where he could hear gunfire, but they weren't shooting at him.

Mikko got the three lookouts' attention a few minutes later and said, "C'mon. We're on the move. Arturo's wounds are not too serious and the cold froze the blood on his head and neck."

The six plowed their way along the path without speaking to each other until Dan yelled, "Hey! Are we going to talk about this?" They were already a mile away from where all of the action had taken place. Mikko and Jaako, who were now in the lead, paused briefly and went off the path into a cluster of small bushes. The rest followed until Mikko came to a rock and slowly stopped. Dan asked another question. "What the hell was all that?"

Mikko was the first to answer. "That was a beginner's mistake and I'm not a beginner at this." The three brothers looked as if they knew immediately what he was talking about. "When we put the scopes on the Russians, we should have taken them off of the rifles first. Somebody saw us pointing our weapons at the patrol and decided to either stop us or scare us." Mikko shook his head. "I can't believe I did that. I just wasn't thinking.

There's no way that there should have been any other soldiers out there. This area isn't a hostile border. They must have known we were here the whole time."

Dan thought for a moment and then spoke. "There's got to be a reason why they've been tracking us. Something really important is happening out here."

The group all looked around at each other before Pete asked a couple of questions. "What do we do now? Should we go back to the car?"

Both Mikko and Jaako said, "Yes."

Mikko said, "There's a small medical kit in the car and we need to make sure Arturo's wounds stay clean. We know the Russians are up to something." He then said something to Jaako in their native tongue and the two of them reached for their poles. Jaako headed back to where they had just been shot at and Mikko headed towards the path. Everyone else was confused. Mikko eventually stopped and said, "Jaako is going to try to take another look at the Russians by himself. He'll be harder to spot alone. We have to be sure that they're not going to follow us. The rest of us should head back to the SUV."

As they made their way to the SUV, Dan wondered if the vehicle was still there. What if the Russians grabbed it? Even if it meant crossing the border illegally, why would they care? They had already fired their weapons across the border into Finland. Dan's concern was eased once he saw Mikko and Pete stop and remove their snow-shoes. Dan had slowed down a few minutes earlier to make sure Arturo and Aleksi were doing okay. When he saw the other two men pick up their snow gear, he moved ahead quickly.

There was the vehicle. It was a beautiful sight. Dan removed his snowshoes and afterwards assisted Arturo with his. Pete was leaning against the hood breathing heavily from his snow excursion. He said that it had been a long time since he had slogged it out in the snow this way.

They loaded all of their gear and got into the SUV. Now they only had to wait for Jaako to report back. Mikko drove back out onto the trail and then eventually ended up back on the frozen stream bed. They would wait for Jaako there. Aleksi tended to Arturo's wounds by using alcohol wipes, which made Arturo wince in pain. Mikko was about to radio Jaako to inform him of their new location when a bright flash followed by a faint boom surprised the men. The sudden occurrence appeared to be located in the area where they had spotted the Russians. The first thought that came to everyone's mind was Jaako.

Without any further hesitation, the men rolled out of the SUV quickly and started out without wearing their snowshoes. They moved in the direction of where they thought Jaako would be. Worrisome looks were all over each man's face. They all thought that Jaako had been attacked by the Russians.

Eventually, their biggest fear was over when they saw Jaako rushing towards them. It was as if he was using his snowshoes as skis. He yelled, "Get back in the car! Get back in the car!" The five hesitated until they saw Jaako remove his snowshoes and abandon them in the snow. They all hopped into the SUV. Mikko drove off quickly.

Finally, Dan summoned the courage to ask Jaako what had happened. Jaako took several breaths before he replied, "I saw the Russians sitting on their machines as if they hadn't shot at us at all. They weren't looking in my direction either. I was about to come back and let you guys know that we didn't have to move so quickly anymore, when something happened that told me that we had to run away. All of a sudden, a bright flash blinded me and a loud sound made me drop down to the ground. When the smoke cleared seconds later, all of the Russians were gone."

Dan chimed in again, "You mean, they left?"

"No," Jaako answered. "They're gone. As in dead. As in incinerated."

The five were completely at a loss for words. Whatever power was now at play, was powerful enough to obliterate man and machine in an instant.

Dan asked the group, "What's our next move?"

After a few moments had passed, Mikko said, "We go back to where our snowmobiles are and rethink our plans. I don't think it's a good idea to go anywhere near the fell or see the bodies today. I have no idea what just happened and it's hard to say if the Russians have any more soldiers tracking us."

No one disagreed with his logic. Very few words were said the rest of the way to the tiny cabin where their machines were hopefully waiting.

10

THE COMPANY YOU KEEP

The SUV was closing in on the cabin when Pete yelled, "Smoke!" Mikko didn't slow down at all. He pulled up to the front of the cabin, but it was no longer there. It was just a smoldering black frame of a house. The men jumped out with their rifles at the ready and immediately headed to the shed in back, which was still intact. Opening the doors, they saw that their six snow machines were gone. Jaako, Dan and Aleksi quickly turned and went to the cabin to see if there were any bodies in it. Finding none, they turned and started to follow the marks left in the snow from the machines. The three men soon returned when they realized that their pursuit was futile. Everyone was thinking the same thoughts. Who took them? What do we do now?

Mikko called everyone into the shed. He stepped outside briefly to fire up a gasoline generator that he knew was in the back of the building. Coming back inside, he plugged in an electric heater that was there and turned on an overhead light. "Close the doors. We need to talk." Pete and Aleksi closed the doors and the group made a semi-circle around Mikko as he was about to speak. "Look, I don't really know what's happening here. I have a few guesses as to who took our snow machines and torched the cabin. That's all it would be, a few guesses."

Dan asked, "Well. What do you think?"

Mikko looked back at him, took a slight breath and gave his assessment. "Number one, it could be rivals of the owners of this place. Let's just say that they are sometimes involved in not-so-legal businesses that can have enemies. Two, somebody could be on to us and is doing their best to disrupt whatever they think we're doing. Or three, somebody randomly came upon this place, saw that nobody was around and stole whatever they could."

"I don't think it was a simple robbery and I don't think it was the same people that killed the Russians," Dan said.

"Why not?" Pete asked.

Dan took a step back so that he could address the whole group. "Well, first of all, there were six snowmobiles. There would have had to have been a fairly large group of them. I would guess six or more. Most opportunistic thieves don't usually travel in big packs. When Aleksi, Jaako and I went over to what was left of the cabin, there was burned food, clothing and pretty much mostly anything that a backwoods cabin would contain, which means that it wasn't your basic ransacking. They would have broken into it and taken anything they could get their hands on. We can also rule out the superpower that erased the Russians, whoever that was would have leveled this entire area."

Pete interrupted him. "The cabin went up quickly and it was no longer burning when we got back. We weren't gone all that long. How could somebody have gotten here, moved the machines out of the way first, lit the fire and then left. And then the fire destroys the place completely. Then, it burns out completely leaving just a little smoke."

Dan agreed. "Exactly. Which means it was a controlled burn. Nothing else was damaged. The shed was fine. The surrounding trees weren't touched. I'd say they used an accelerant." He stopped to see if anyone had a response and Arturo did. Arturo nodded in agreement with Dan's assessment. Dan nodded back and continued with his theory. "I've written a few articles on notorious business tycoons who deliberately destroyed a building or two using fire. In a couple of these crimes an accelerant like butane, kerosene or even a liquid like turpentine was used to speed up the burn process. Common thieves who want to destroy do not usually take the time to do that, and then stick around to make sure that it doesn't spread. I bet if we go over to the cabin remains right now, we'll see unusual burn patterns, melted material and maybe some weird coloration on some of the items that didn't burn completely."

Dan continued. "I think that this heist was planned and burning the cabin was a statement. It could be from the rivals of your friends, Mikko, but I've got a weird feeling it was someone else, who wanted to make a statement for sure and they wanted to slow us down too. They could have waited and killed us, but they didn't. That's why I don't think it was done by rival criminals. But I do realize that this vehicle we're using would be a nice addition to their collection."

"Not if they were trying to draw the least amount of attention to themselves," Mikko replied. "Stealing and driving around the SUV would have drawn all kinds of attention from people around here, especially my acquaintances."

Dan agreed. "That's my point. I think someone else knows we're up to something that's secretive and they're trying to screw it up for us. I just can't understand why they don't just kill us."

Mikko checked his watch and brought up another issue to the group. "It's getting late. I think that we should stay in this shed for the night instead of going back to my house. We have bedding, food and guns. Whoever did this won't likely think that we would stick around, so that's exactly what we should do. Dan, why don't you and Pete go check out the cabin and see if you can find out if any accelerants were used, just so we know what we're dealing with. The rest of us will unload the SUV and organize the gear. Then I'll radio my wife and tell her that we're staying here, so she won't worry. By the way, everybody take off their white clothing. We're going dark again."

Everybody agreed and got started on their tasks. Sleeping bags were laid out on the wooden floor of the shed on top of some old mats that were found in the small loft above. Packs were put next to each person's sleeping area. Mikko and Aleksi found some chains hanging on the back wall of the shed. Mikko told everyone around him in Finnish, "These are chains for tires. Let's see if they fit our SUV. It doesn't matter if we make noise now because people seem to know that we're in the area. It'll be easier and safer to use them because a portion of the trip back to my house may not be too passable by automobile if we get snow or high winds that cause snowdrifts."

Jaako volunteered and Arturo, feeling only a stinging sensation from his wounds, offered to do the same. He was quickly overruled by Aleksi, who wanted him to take it easy. Arturo relented and went back to arranging the gear in the shed. Mikko took out a few more items from the back of the SUV and then said, "I've got to call my wife, before it gets real late." He took a walkie talkie from the vehicle and walked away from the rest of the group, sensing that his wife would not be happy about his predicament.

Meanwhile, Dan and Pete were sifting through the sad remnants of the cabin. Dan pointed out the inconsistent burn patterns. He reached down and carefully picked up a still warm leg of a chair. He put his nose near it and called Pete over to him. "Smell this."

Pete took a slight whiff and said, "It kinda smells like bad vodka."

Dan gave a slight grin and replied, "It's isopropyl alcohol. Rubbing alcohol. My guess is that somebody probably figured that it wouldn't leave many stains and that it had a much weaker smell."

The two went back to the rest of the group to tell them what they had found. By this time, the gear was completely unpacked, Mikko had returned from his call to his wife and the SUV was jacked up and getting fitted for its chain shoes. Mikko had joined Jaako and Aleksi at the vehicle and was helping with the front tires. He stopped when Dan and Pete walked near him. He asked, "What did you find?"

Dan shrugged his shoulders and said, "Isopropyl alcohol."

Mikko didn't look surprised. "Makes sense. There's a real need out here for it. It's used for wounds, antifreeze and some crazies even mix it with other alcohol for a supercharged kind of liquor. It's their version of your American moonshine, except we call it a Molotov cocktail, like the homemade grenades."

Dan and Pete lent a hand with the tires and after fitting the back tires with the chains, the five men went into the shed. They noticed that the generator in back was off and Arturo had lit a fire inside the shed. They were about to yell at him, but he diffused the situation by saying, "I know. I know. Why didn't I leave the generator on? First of all, there's not enough gasoline for it to run all night. Secondly, the generator makes too much noise. I know, Mikko. You said it doesn't matter, and people already know we're out here. But you also said that nobody would think that we would spend the night here either. Why take a chance on drawing too much attention to ourselves? I found this solid metal bin and dragged it to the middle of the floor. There were some flat stones piled up on the side of this shed. They were stuck frozen to each other, but I pried them loose and set the bin on top of them, so hopefully the wooden floor won't heat up too much. There are so many holes and spaces in the walls and ceiling, that I don't think we have to worry about the smoke."

They were all astonished. Arturo had laid out their bedding, carried a bunch of rocks inside and dragged a bin over to the center of the floor. He then gathered firewood and even had it ablaze when they walked through the doors.

Aleksi walked over to him and said, "Thanks, you idiot. Let's see if you did anything to your wounds." He looked at Arturo's scalp and saw that the head wound bandage was fine. Looking at the neck bandage, he noticed a small stream of blood trickling below it. He took an alcohol wipe from the med kit and wiped it clean. He didn't say a word. He just slapped Arturo on his left shoulder blade and pointed his finger at him. Arturo lifted up his two arms pretending that he didn't know that he had done something wrong.

Each man put a rifle next to their sleeping bag. They all kept a pistol and knife strapped to their waist. They sat up on their sleeping bags and began to converse with one another about what had transpired that day and what would be their next plan of action.

Mikko said, "My wife wasn't too happy about us not coming home tonight. She will have food waiting for us whenever we do arrive and plenty of sheets and pillows out in case we need to rest. Since the snowmobiles are gone, we will have to rely on the SUV to travel from place to place. It needs to be recharged at my place and that will take many hours."

Jaako said, "Each man should take a turn at keeping watch over the rest of us while we sleep in case some unfriendlies show up during the night."

Everyone agreed that each man would take an hour of guard duty, starting after they finished eating. Each man doing one hour would bring the time to about six o'clock in the morning. The last man on duty could fall asleep at six because no one thought that any bad guys would plan an attack on them right around the time that many people were awakening.

Mikko would take the first watch, followed by Arturo, Pete, Dan, Jaako and then Aleksi. The men ate their survival food, traded stories and then five of them went to sleep. Mikko moved to sit on a crate at a window that was cracked open a little because of the fire. He picked up a few pieces of wood, dropped them into the flames and returned to his window seat. He gave out a sigh and put on a pair of night vision goggles.

By the time it was Dan's turn, it was just after three o'clock. Pete nudged him and he got up immediately, as if he hadn't been asleep. He put on his boots and grabbed his rifle. He had slept in his jacket and gloves. He put on his black ski mask, his night vision glasses and decided to go outside because he felt nature calling. It was snowing and extremely cold. He had hoped that he could have held on until the sun came up many hours later. The frigid temperature hit him hard when he exited the building. As he headed towards the nearest tree, he thought he saw a quick flash of light coming from the area of where the cabin had once stood. He felt suddenly pulled in two different directions. His original duty was to keep watch over his group. Now he sensed something else was amiss.

The answer to his quandary tapped him on the shoulder nearly causing him to relieve himself right on the spot. It was Pete and Jaako. Pete whispered, "What's going on? We thought we heard you running."

Dan calmed himself and said in a low voice, "I saw a flash in the woods near the now deceased cabin." The three stood still for a moment, contemplating their next move.

Their decision was made when Mikko joined them. "Aleksi and Arturo are awake and staying with the SUV. What are you guys doing out here?" he asked. "I heard you stomping in the snow."

Pete said, "Dan thought he saw a light out here somewhere."

Mikko motioned to the other three to move to the side of the shed. Even though they couldn't see them very well, they knew that Aleksi and Arturo were behind the vehicle about fifty feet away. Mikko waved to them using a tiny flashlight and extended his left arm to tell them to stay put. He began whispering to the three next to him. "Dan and I will go to the right of the cabin. You two go to the left. Be sure to stay within the treeline to cover your movements. I hope everyone has their night visions with them."

Jaako whispered, "What do we do if we see something?"

Mikko thought for a moment. "We play it by ear. Depends on who or what it is."

The four split up and headed for the treelines that surrounded the property. The snow was semi-crusty and was somewhat noisy to walk on if they hurried. The men walked slowly until they got to the trees where the snow was still mostly powder. Dan spotted the light again and tapped Mikko on the shoulder. He pointed past Mikko and both of them watched the light move quickly as if it was scanning the area. Mikko pulled his night vision glasses out and slipped them on over his ski mask.

Soon, they were all wearing their own. They started moving towards the last place they thought the light was. Guns drawn, they moved steadily but carefully in the now falling snow. As they got within seventy feet of their destination, they heard a noise where the other two should have been. Seconds later, they heard a popping noise where they had been headed. A moment later, shots rang out from Pete's and Jaako's supposed position. Dan and Mikko instinctively dropped to the ground.

A pair of headlights appeared behind them. It was Aleksi and Arturo. They had decided to wait in the vehicle to stay warm. When they heard the gunfire, Aleksi turned the silent machine's lights on and the two of them headed towards the action on foot. The outside four moved in from both sides with their rifles pointed in the direction they were all traveling. The snow and wind were pounding them at this point, but still they pressed forward.

Aleksi and Arturo had joined in the fun by moving down the middle. Nobody at this point bothered to walk quietly. They walked as quickly as possible, but found no sign of anyone or anything. The snow and wind were becoming too much for them, so Mikko ran back to the SUV and then drove back to the five. Rolling down the window, he yelled, "Two of you get in! The rest stay here!"

Dan and Jaako jumped in the back and Mikko sped out to the road. Stopping, they got out quickly and scanned the area. They saw snow-filled tire marks, but they couldn't tell whether they were theirs from earlier or newly made. Disgusted, Mikko went back to the vehicle, followed by Dan and Jaako. When they arrived back at the shed, the others were already there.

"What just happened?" Mikko asked Pete and Jaako. "What were you guys shooting at?"

Pete gave his excuse. "I started it. I thought someone was shooting at us and I returned fire. Jaako only fired because I did."

Dan asked, "What made you think someone was shooting at you?"

Pete said, "Didn't you hear the popping sound? It sounded like small weapons fire."

Jaako added, "Or maybe somebody using a makeshift suppressor."

They discussed their options and came to the conclusion that whoever it was, they were not likely to come back right away.

Mikko pointed out, "We might as well all get some sleep. They know that we're willing to use our weapons. Unless they come back with an army, we should be good."

Dan watched as the other five went to their individual bed rolls. He had other plans. Nature was still calling him. He motioned to Pete and Mikko and they understood. Back out into the cold he went to finish his original mission. He hoped

he would complete it without any further interrup-
tions.

John Alan
he would complete it without any further interrup-
tions.

106

11

BACK TO SQUARE ONE

The six began to stir at around six-thirty, beginning with Mikko, then Dan and the rest. Sunrise in the morning in Lapland during this time of year was virtually nonexistent. Closer to the noon hour, the sun pushes up over the horizon and then dips below it a couple hours or so later lingering below the horizon line for a good portion of what are normal daylight hours everywhere else. Although dark, if there is a clear moonlit sky and clean sparkling snow, then it's not too dark to move around easily much like dawn or dusk.

Everyone moved quickly without speaking, packed up their gear and loaded the SUV in around twenty minutes. Mikko had radioed his wife Katriina to let her know that they were on their way. She said, "Breakfast will be waiting when you arrive."

They all agreed to say little to Katriina about their ordeal. They would explain Arturo's wounds as nothing more than him accidentally dropping his own rifle and shooting himself. He was taking one for the team by pretending to be a clumsy idiot.

The ride to Mikko's house was very interesting because the trails, paths and roads in that area were meant to be traveled by snow machines during the winter. Despite all of the possible road hazards, they arrived at Mikko's house around mid-morning. Breakfast was nearly ready, so the men hurried to unpack their gear. They didn't take everything out, because they figured that they would be back in that same vehicle later, due to the loss of their snowmobiles. They all briefly washed up before sitting down and were enjoying a nice late breakfast.

Mikko's children had already eaten and were bouncing around from person to person seeking attention. They didn't get many visitors due to their remote lifestyle. When they did, they usually pestered the guests relentlessly because they never knew when they were going to see them or anybody again. The cabin was tiny but comfortable. There was barely enough room to fit the six men around the table. Katriina would pass them a bowl or platter of something and each man would pass it along after taking some food. Katriina would then take the bowl or platter back because there wasn't enough space at the table to set it down.

After everyone had eaten, Dan and Pete helped bring the dishes and utensils over to the sink. Katriina was pleasantly surprised that American men would pitch in to do chores. They both offered to help wash and dry the plates, cups and dinnerware, but Katriina would have none of it. "Go sit down and relax. You've had a strenuous twenty-four hours." Dan and Pete obeyed and went into the next room where the rest of their party had retired. The other four were discussing their next plan in Finnish. When the two Americans entered the cramped sitting room, the conversation changed to English.

Mikko said, "Here's what we should do. I hooked up the SUV to our gas generator where it will take several hours to recharge. We'll lose all of the good part of the day, so we'll stay here tonight. Tomorrow, we get up by six and leave right after breakfast." He looked at Pete and his cousins and said, "We head to your grandparents. The road to their house is better than anything we were on before, but it will still be hazardous. If everything goes smoothly, we can take a look at the bodies and then a quick glance at the fell. We'd have to head right back to your grandparents' house because it would be late by that time."

The cousins all nodded in agreement. Mikko suggested that they begin the process of taking a shower one by one. With the cabin's lone bathroom and six men needing to use it, the amount of time needed to complete this process could be well over an hour. Water was a luxury and it was not uncommon in this part of Finland for wells to dry up at various times of the year. Mikko asked that everyone limit their shower time to five minutes. The cabin contained an adequate wood burning hot water system, but with this many people, Mikko was most concerned about water usage. There was an outhouse or *ulkohuussi* in the back of the property, but it was bitterly cold and had no bathing facilities.

Dan and Pete opted to wait until the end of the shower line. For the time being, they decided to take a walk outside. It was late morning and the sun was just starting to make its way up to just below the horizon. It was a clear day and fairly pleasant as far as winter days in Lapland went. They hadn't had a chance to talk alone since arriving in Finland.

Dan asked, "So what's the story about *The Mob's* possible buyout by the *New York Times*?

Pete said, "Doug Pearson accidentally heard information, which he passed on to me. When I asked Roger for further details, he told me to keep it to myself and then looked at me like I was an idiot. That look confirmed what Doug told me."

Dan was also trying to find out if Pete knew anything more about this story. He didn't doubt that there was a story worthy of telling. After all, here he was only in Finland for about two days and he had already been shot at from across the border by Russians. Dan just had a feeling that there was something more at hand. Pete didn't provide him with any more information, which made Dan come to a couple of conclusions. Either Pete was in the dark about a lot of things or he was holding back for some important reason. Dan was hoping that it was the former.

The two reporters continued their walk. Their conversation shifted to the beauty of Finland and the uniqueness of the region. Dan asked questions about Pete's grandparents. "How are they faring out here? This has got to be a hard life for older people, no?"

"The way of life way out here and near the Korvatunturi Fell is tough for anyone, no matter what age they are," Pete said. When they turned to head back to the cabin, Pete pulled on Dan's arm, "Look over there." Then he pointed to the impending sunrise. It was a clear sky, save for a few clouds in the background. Even though the sun was still a ways off from showing itself over the eastern horizon, its light peeked out over the surrounding hills. The two men marveled at how the light reflected off the clouds behind. They said not a word. It was perfectly quiet all around them, except for the faint moaning of Mikko's gas generator.

Dan got to thinking about the possible dangers that lay in front of them, remembering what they had already been through the day and night before. He was going to be heading deeper into the wilderness towards the mysterious fell, probably towards a more treacherous unknown. "I'd like to talk with you more Pete but it's so stinkin' cold out here."

Pete understood as he and Dan calmly spun around and walked to the front door of the Kurtti residence. Pete went in first. Dan stopped and faced the faint light. He thought about the dead bodies that were on the horizon of his little group, then he turned and went into the warmth and safety of the cabin.

The men spent the rest of the day mostly helping around the house, having fun with the little ones and getting their gear ready for their next adventure. The children were homeschooled and each adult took a turn assisting with their lessons. Dan and Pete helped with English grammar and sentence structure. After dinner, the men helped with the cleanup. Then the five visitors unfurled their bedrolls anywhere they could find room in the tiny abode, which ended up being on two sofas, a reasonably comfortable old recliner and the floor. At first both Aleksi and Arturo said, "I call shotgun on a sofa!"

Then Katriina stepped in with a firm voice. "Oh no you don't. They're for our guests, you know, our real guests."

The children went to bed by eight and the grownups sat around idly chatting about Finland, the United States, Russia and China, until it was their bedtime too. The six men, however, ended up staying awake long after Mikko's family had fallen asleep. Mikko had brought out some viina, which was a clear spirit drink that he and some of his friends had distilled on their own. Dan was no stranger to imbibing, but this hit him pretty hard. Pete wasn't much better off, but they managed to hang in there with the local boys. It was around midnight when the moonshine shindig ended; morning would come quickly.

They all looked at each other and in unison said, "Goodnight." Then they rose to their feet at the same time and made their way to their prospective sleeping bags. Dan settled in, but he couldn't shake the feeling that Pete was withholding valuable information from him. He only hoped that any crucial intel that was being withheld would present itself before it was too late.

12

A NEW-FOUND APPRECIATION

Morning did indeed come quickly. The six were all up and moving around by six o'clock. Some were slower than usual because of the festivities of the night before, but once they brought their gear outside, the cold air shook them awake. The SUV was packed in ten minutes and food was on the table when they went back inside. They ate in a hurry and, as always, helped tidy up the place before leaving. Goodbyes and thank you's were exchanged with Mikko's family. Mikko lagged behind the other five in order to say a private farewell to Katriina and the children. He eventually climbed into the vehicle last, and without hesitation, started the silent motor and headed for the Sironen residence.

It was a slow but steady process. The SUV still had chains on its tires, but the road they traveled was narrow. Mikko did all that he could to avoid scraping the doors on trees and anything else that was on the sides of the road. He was successful for about half an hour, until the road narrowed to a point where the panels on the right side started peeling off like dead skin on a sunburned body. Steering the SUV became nearly impossible due to trees, rocky outcrops and deep snow, which had fallen the day before. Mikko was not expecting all of these land traps, but he held it together until the steering totally went. The auto veered to the right, went off the road when it widened and slid awkwardly into the woods. It came to a stop on its own. The six looked around at each other as if to make sure nobody was hurt. When it was confirmed that everybody was safe and sound, they all got out to assess the damage.

Mikko knew they were in trouble. He felt it in the steering mechanism. They didn't have the tools to fix it, so he took out his walkie talkie and said, "I'm calling for roadside assistance." The men all smiled at Mikko's joke.

He actually contacted the cousins' grandfather. Like many of the residents near the fell, Frans and Katri Sironen had a radio because no cell towers existed for many miles. Katri answered because Frans was outside working on the generators that provided power to the rather large log cabin they lived in with their only granddaughter.

Frans and Katri were both seventy-five years old, but they looked and acted at least fifteen years younger. Frans was a strong, sturdy, bull of a man and Katri was nearly the same. She looked like she could hold her own in a bar fight, but she had a great smile and a pretty face. Despite Frans' spryness and endless energy, Katri often worried about him and hoped that he would slow down a bit.

When Mikko's call came in, Katri went outside and called out to Frans to man the radio. While this call was being made, the other men looked at the damage to the SUV and determined that it was hopeless. The area of the forest that they had fallen into was thick, but opened up about a hundred yards from the road. Dan, Pete and Jaako decided to explore their surroundings as Mikko talked to Frans. They wore their snowshoes, carried poles and slung rifles over their shoulders. It took them five minutes to reach the opening. When they got there, they looked around and nearly fell over because of what they saw.

Jaako was the youngest of the three, so Dan and Pete volunteered him to go back and get the others. Dan and Pete both took a knee for a minute or so before they removed their snowshoes and moved closer to the objects of their attention. Covered by heavy white tarps were the six missing snowmobiles. They pulled the canvas pieces off and both men instinctively got on one each and started them up. By the time the other men had joined them, they had ridden towards them and circled around like little kids who had just gotten new toys. Everyone else jumped on one and headed towards the SUV. When they all had stopped and turned the engines off, all eyes focused on Mikko. They pounded him with who, what and why questions.

The best answer he could give was, "The thieves hid the machines and planned on retrieving them at a more convenient time." Mikko then said to the group, "We've got to get out of here ASAP, but we can't leave the auto because they'll take it as a consolation prize."

Pete's grandfather wasn't due for at least an hour, so they decided to bring all of the snowmobiles to the side of the road and check to see if each one was still fully functioning. Then they anxiously waited to be rescued, hopefully by someone who was friendly.

13

THE EYES HAVE IT

Less than an hour later, the sound of a large vehicle could be heard pushing through the soft snow. From a distance, the vehicle was green in color and looked like a cross between a Humvee and a half-track armored vehicle from World War II. Due to its wide wheelbase, it was banging into everything on the sides of the road but the driver didn't seem to pay the minor collisions any mind, because the behemoth kept coming. All of the men drew their weapons, but it kept heading towards them.

Mikko was the first to lower his rifle. As he did so, he started laughing. He knew who it was immediately. Aleksi and Arturo had already lowered theirs as the vehicle came closer to them. They too were laughing. Pete and Dan were still holding their rifles steady, as if frozen in time. When they finally snapped out of their trances, they realized that Mikko and Jaako were heading towards the driver's side door. Pete said to Dan, "Must be my grandfather." He too began making his way to the door.

Dan stood back to take it all in because he felt like an outsider. He was waiting to see a tank of an elderly man exit the vehicle. Instead, he was treated to seeing a tall attractive blonde. Some grandfather, he laughingly thought. He was eventually introduced to the granddaughter, Kirsti.

Pete got Dan's attention. "Dan, this is my cousin Kirsti Anna Sironen." Kirsti Anna Sironen, Dan repeated in his mind. What a beautiful name for the most beautiful woman in the world. A parade of music was sent spiraling out of control in his thoughts. With all of this going on in his head, he forgot to say hello.

Kirsti had reached for his hand, but he had no idea that he had reached back. She said in the most beautiful voice he had ever heard, "It's a pleasure to meet you."

All Dan could muster was, "Hey there Kirsti. You have nice blue eyes. I mean, you look very nice." Pete glared at him hoping he would explode.

She politely smiled and said, "Thank you Dan."

She then turned and hugged Mikko, Pete and her brother Jaako. Arturo and Aleksi came slogging along and joined in the hug fest with their sister. Kirsti said, "I came instead of Pappa. Mummi wanted him to stay and work on the generators." She was, of course, referring to her grandparents.

Mikko spoke to her in Finnish. Dan figured that he was either explaining that they would have to tow the SUV behind the Humvee on steroids, or that the American was an idiot and don't worry about his lack of couth. Dan's thoughts were interrupted when the passenger side door suddenly opened revealing yet another blonde beauty stepping out onto the snow. She greeted everyone in Finnish.

Before Dan could make a fool of himself again, Pete jumped into the mix and said to him, "Dan, this is Livia." Pete then put his arm around Livia, faced Dan and gave him a look of death in order to keep his mind on earth.

Dan got the message loud and clear. This time, he said something much more in tune with him being an intelligent journalist. "Hi."

Pete waited for him to follow that with something uncomfortable, but it didn't happen. She said to Dan, "Call me Liv." He smiled and nodded.

She was a distant neighbor to Kirsti and her grandparents. Liv and Kirsti had gone to college together, both majoring in engineering. They didn't know each other very well until college, but now they were joined at the hip.

By now, it was late morning. The sun was up as high as it would be for the rest of the day. The entire group got to work. The women took out a homemade apparatus used to tow automobiles. Kirsti got back in the driver's seat, while Liv and

Mikko attached the rig to the back of the half-track. Upon their command, she backed up the vehicle to the SUV. Because the injured vehicle was off the side of the road, Kirsti had to work at maneuvering the half-track just right. In any case, time was of the essence because the threat of an unknown enemy was still very real.

Everything was ready within twenty minutes. Kirsti led the way in the armored monster. Mikko piloted the SUV. Even though his vehicle was disabled, he was needed in the driver's seat to use his foot on the brake if the SUV started moving too much to one side. The towing device was just a little better than using a towing chain, so Mikko had a dangerous task ahead of him due to the icy layer below the snow. Mikko was followed by the six snowmobiles with Liv now driving one of them. Liv rode next to Dan, much to his liking. It took an hour to get to the Sironen patriarch's cabin and was still light when they arrived and Pappa Frans was outside to greet them. He had finished working on the generators and had cleaned off the solar panels in order to take advantage of the precious sunlight that was not going to last much longer. He was just about to chop wood for the fireplace when the gang pulled up near the front door. He stopped what he was doing and called out to them. "Welkəm!"

Pappa Frans greeted everyone with hugs and handshakes, including Dan. He spoke mostly

Finnish, but had a decent command of the English language. Mummi Katri was inside preparing food and setting the table in the surprisingly spacious log home.

When Mikko showed Frans the damaged SUV, he asked him in Finnish, "Do you think you can fix it?"

Frans said to him in English, "I can fix almost anything!"

Katri came outside and embraced all of the newcomers and quickly ushered all but Frans, Kirsti and Liv inside. Frans motioned to Kirsti and Liv to bring the two largest vehicles around back. Dan and Pete came back outside to help put the snowmobiles in the large shed that stood next to a barn near the treeline. It was warm inside both buildings. Kirsti and Liv brought the halftrack and SUV to the front of the barn, opened the doors and then disappeared inside with the vehicles.

Frans had rigged up an outdoor wood burning furnace that provided ample heat to both structures. The barn contained a second floor with a rustic but comfortable living area and had a tiny kitchen, comfortable sofas, and a bathroom with a shower. Cots that were normally stored in a closet, were opened up with a blanket and pillow on each. Mikko and the brothers would sleep there. Dan and Pete, although they had assured their hosts that they would be perfectly fine in the barn with the rest of their troupe, were overruled by Katri. "You are new guests. You stay in the house."

Once all of the machinery was put away, everyone congregated inside the house, which was a work of art. Dan learned that Frans and some of his friends had renovated it twenty-five years ago because the structure had been in the family for many decades and fallen into disrepair. Frans and Katri, at the time, were living in their own little house outside the fell's national park region. Not wanting the place to fall into ruin, Frans and Katri moved into the barn that would soon be occupied by Mikko and the brothers that night. Frans would work on the house with whatever friends were available. If the place remained unlivable and unoccupied, the family would have had to sell it to the government. Frans was too stubborn to let that happen. After the project was completed over a period of three years, he and Katri decided to retire there.

Over the years, the brothers and Kirsti would visit and be put to work. Mikko spent some time there too. Helping one another was quite common and quite necessary in this part of the country. It was a hard life with the hard outside elements constantly at play. Even though most neighbors were almost always miles apart from each other, the settlers in this region relied on one another to survive. People exchanged food, supplies and skills to make a life out here in the wilderness. Kirsti would eventually move in to help the aging grandparents maintain the residence. She would later be hired by the government as an engineer, along with Liv. Both were lucky to be assigned to positions just ninety minutes away. To an outsider, ninety minutes seemed like an eternity to travel. To the residents of the park, it was well…like a walk in the park.

14

WHATEVER GETS YOU THROUGH THE NIGHT

Everyone made their way to the dining room after washing up a bit. Pappa Frans sat down at the end of the table and gestured for everyone to sit. Mummi Katri gave him such a look, which prompted him to get up and get the pitcher of fresh cow's milk from the cold box in an unheated but insulated porch off the kitchen. He also grabbed a container of water and placed them on the table.

By this time, the only person standing was Katri. She carried in a large tray of Kalakukko, a traditional food of Finland consisting of fish along with pork baked inside of bread. In this case, the fish of choice was herring. Dan was the only one unfamiliar with this kind of food. If he was nervous about whether his pallet could tolerate this Finnish fare, he didn't let on to anyone. He saw food that he recognized in the form of potatoes and carrots.

He reached for the potatoes, but he was intercepted by Kirsti placing a serving of the fish bread on his plate. He looked down at it apprehensively, but as he looked up and into her eyes, he forgot that he was even in Finland.

He thanked her and then continued towards the potatoes. When his plate was full of food, he took a stab at the fish. He decided to rip the Band-Aid off and he dug right into the unknown. His first taste was strong, given the fact that it was herring. As he ate more, he got used to it and actually took a second portion. The vegetables were a nice yin to the fish's yang. They were subtle in taste and complimented the Kalakukko quite nicely.

A side effect of the main course was that, afterwards, Dan felt as if he had just eaten an American Thanksgiving meal, full almost to the point of extreme pain and he wanted to go lie down somewhere for hours. The potatoes and carrots wouldn't be his savior because they had a habit of sticking to his gills too.

Katri wouldn't allow the six men to assist in the cleanup. Instead, she kicked them and the two young women out of the dining area. She did manage to detain Frans by saying in Finnish, "Hei! Minne luulet meneväsi?" Which basically meant, "Hey! Where do you think you're going?" Frans protested briefly and seeing that he was about to lose the battle anyway, he picked up some plates from the table and brought them into the kitchen.

Eventually, they were able to join the lads and ladies around the fireplace.

Frans brought in some viina, which Dan had already been introduced to two days earlier. After everyone had received a glass, they drank a toast. Dan was amazed at how calm the other members of the group of six were. Jaako had witnessed a terrifying event. They had all been shot at and Arturo had been hit twice, but here they were talking, laughing and drinking as if it was just another day. Dan was anxious to know more about what was going on, but surprisingly, a sense of calm was hanging over him too. He didn't want to ruin the mood, but he had to ask, "What's the plan for tomorrow?"

Frans answered him, "Today, we make sure your snowmobiles are filled with petrol and that you have all of the equipment you need. Tomorrow, you will follow me and I will take you to see the bodies. I hope you are not, how do I say it in English, squeamish."

Katri was not interested in the conversation. She got up from sitting on the arm of Frans' chair and headed to the kitchen. When Kirsti and Liv went to join her, she stopped them and said in Finnish, "Stay. You probably need to hear what's going on. I do not." The two young women stayed. They would be joining the trek for a short time in order to ensure that the men made it to the fell.

Frans continued talking. "Dan, there are things going on in this part of Lapland that are not happening anywhere else in the world. The others, including Pete, are aware of this and it's time to let you know what you are getting into." He had Dan's complete attention. "I will not tell you everything because it would be too much to take in all at once. I'll let Pete or anyone else tell you more."

Frans took a sip of his drink before proceeding. "I have lived in the wilderness for seventy-five years and I don't completely understand it. All of us who have lived in this area around the fell have just accepted things the way that they are, which includes the settlers inside Russia too. Very strange it is. The fell is the centerpiece of all of this."

Dan trolled for more information. "The center of what?"

Frans looked as if he had regretted taking the lead with the story, but none of the other Finns offered him any help. He pushed on with the tale. "You see, the fell has always been the center of mystery dating back centuries. Its ear-shaped formation adds to the mystery. It is said that the fell contains a source of power that can't be understood or imagined by average people." Dan was puzzled, but he remained quiet and attentive. Frans stated unashamedly, "It saved Finland."

"How?" Dan asked.

Frans said. "You see, Suomi, or Finland as you say, had been involved in much conflict over the centuries. Finland battled people from Russia and then the Soviet Union, Germany and even itself. Ancient history has told us that we battled with and against our Scandinavian neighbors. Vikings came and went too. But since the early twentieth century, we have managed to carry on. It's almost as if a higher power has been looking out for us."

"You mean God?" Dan asked.

"If you mean the Almighty, then no. If you mean a power more formidable than the average human, then yes. You see, for centuries things were out of control here. We fought and fought and fought. It was as if there was no end to it. Then magically, our destiny seemed to change overnight. The wars didn't end, but they lessened in number. In 1917, after being dominated by the Russian Empire for so long, and by others before that, we emerged as an independent country. We fought ourselves again in 1918. Germany got involved and it was difficult getting them out, but we did. But unfortunately, we weren't so lucky against the Soviets. We lost part of Suomi known as Karelia to them and have never gotten it back."

Dan added, "The Winter War."

Frans, somewhat gratified that Dan knew the terminology, nodded his head in agreement. "Then, in our quest for revenge, I guess, the powers that be at the time made a deal with the devil."

Dan asked, "Hitler?"

Frans nodded again, "We lost but we learned. When we got ourselves upright again, we fought him and won. We didn't like what happened with the former Soviet Union. We never will. Karelia belongs with us. Maybe someday that issue will be resolved. However, this part of Lapland seems to have been spared. After the Lapland War against the German's ended in 1918, Lapland and the entire country seemed to be at peace. For us living near the fell, we have a connection with the people living right on the border in Russia. Some are Suomi, some are Russian. Whatever happens with us seems to happen to them and, what is the term, vice versa. We don't like their government, but we like the border people. And they like us. It's as if the fell mountain region is its own entity."

Dan proceeded to dig deeper into this higher power matter. He asked, "What is the force and its purpose?"

Frans shrugged his shoulders. "I don't know for sure. I can tell you what I think, but you're going to think I'm crazy."

Dan said, "Okay. Try me."

Frans answered, "Alright, but please don't think that what I'm about to tell you is the ramblings of an old man. There are many near the fell who agree with me. Where do I begin? Well, everyone knows about Norse mythology ever since the Power Rangers movies came out decades or so ago."

Dan was confused until Pete, who had remained silent like the others, politely interceded, "You mean the Avengers movies, Pappa."

Frans looked at him momentarily. "Oh yes, that's it. Now where was I? Those movies made

Thor and Viking myths very popular." He paused and leaned closer to Dan. "Only they're not totally myths." Dan looked around at everyone to see if they had just heard what Frans had said. They looked back at him as if they were looking for his reaction. He looked over at Pete and he had the same look as his fellow Finns, serious and unflinching.

Frans continued with his story. "You see, the story goes that Thor was this great warrior god and I am not contesting that interpretation at all but he wasn't what the movies made him out to be. He was strong, yes, but much more. He was the average person's god. He would have rather solved a conflict with his hammer than with words. He was not without faults. He lost battles and had fallen to the allure of women. He also made many other mistakes. This was why he was adored by the Vikings. He was relentless, despite his shortcomings. As some gods from legend do, he died at the end of the world."

Dan's eyebrows raised. Frans laughed and said, "I know what you are thinking. I said that he died. Yes, but at the end of his world, not ours. Most people would say that he died because Christianity came about. That's also an interpretation. You see, gods received their power from people believing in them. When that belief weakened, so did their power. Legend has it that Thor died shortly after slaying a great serpent and that his sons retrieved his hammer, Mjolnir. The story also says that his sons died later. What is cloudy after that is the whereabouts of the hammer. Some accounts have it being destroyed because Thor and his heirs died, thus taking with them the strong magic that protected the hammer."

Frans took a breather from his dissertation to take a drink and then started back up again. "It is the belief of some older people around here that the hammer was destroyed in the fell, but its magic wasn't. Many of them insist that the hammer broke into many little pieces, each with its own piece of the power remaining. Still, others believe that this power was embedded into the mountain and that's why strange things happen. After we see the bodies tomorrow, I will tell you more of the tale. You can decide for yourself what to believe."

Dan and everyone else remained silent waiting for Dan to start laughing. Dan, instead, decided to ask a question. "Frans, what do you believe?"

Frans looked around before he answered. "I am a very skeptical man. Many of the stories that people around here believe in are the works of silly old men and women. I laugh at the thought of their beliefs." Then, he stopped talking. He stared at Dan for a moment and said, "But, I am an old man too." He then winked at Dan, got up and said, "Everybody, make sure you are prepared for tomorrow. We leave at eight."

Frans walked into the kitchen and was quickly corralled into helping Katri with housework. The rest of the gang got up and went about preparing for the next day. Supplies were checked and added to when needed. The snowmobiles were looked over to see if any repairs were necessary. Except for a few new scratches, everything seemed ready to go. Weapons, ammunition, night vision goggles, walkie talkies, snowshoes, poles, food, water, rope and survival camping gear were carefully piled onto each snowmobile.

The plan was that Frans, Kirsti and Liv would ride in the half-track, followed by the six men on their recaptured snowmobiles. They would examine the bodies, which were stowed away on the property of a friend of Frans'. Dan and Pete would examine, photograph and take videos of the evidence. Then, the six would continue on towards the fell, where they would dismount and trek up the mountain and into the lowlands inside.

Their purpose for going up and into the fell was still not completely clear to Dan. He knew that they were going to investigate the strange glow that was sometimes being emitted from the mountain. He guessed that the bodies had been recovered from that area too, but nothing about that had been said yet. Normally, he would have grilled Pete's family for this information, but he sensed that some things were being held back from him. Even though Frans seemed to really stick his neck out and tell a tall tale that most people would call delusional and ridiculous, Dan had seen the expressions on the faces of his Finnish family, and they weren't laughing. Something was up and he was just waiting for his news story to develop in front of him.

After all of the preparations had been completed, Dan decided to take a walk. By this time, the sunlight was fading under the midday clouds. He asked Kirsti if she would show him around the property and she said that she and Liv would be happy to give him a tour. Normally, Dan would have felt slighted with the inclusion of a second person, but being in the presence of two beautiful women eased the pain. They put on their winter outerwear and walked out the door.

The three of them talked about their jobs, hobbies and what they did for excitement. The ladies were both intrigued and amused by Dan's portrayal of life in a big city. Neither of the women had ever been to New York, but both had been to Boston a few years back. They had an American college friend living there and she took them around the city and surrounding area for a week. They told Dan that they had enjoyed the culture and nightlife of Boston and the slow pace of Cape Cod. Dan told them that he had never been to Finland and that he would like to come back during the summertime to see more of the country when there were more hours of daylight. The three of them laughed at the same time.

Kirsti wasn't leading the trio in any certain direction, but she said, "Let's go to the observation deck so that you can see for miles before there is no sun left." They walked up a slight hill and came upon a structure that looked something like a glorified lifeguard's chair. It was tall with a ladder attached to one side. Up at the top, there was a flat railing going around a somewhat sturdy floor.

As they were about to climb, a voice shouted, "Hey, do you have room for a fourth?" It was Pete. He had spotted the three leaving while he was still putting together his equipment and had finally caught up to them. Dan would have usually been annoyed with a guy ambushing his stroll with a woman, but since there were two of them, it didn't make much of a difference. They waved him over and started their advance up the ladder, ladies first.

When they got to the top, they were overlooking a winter wonderland. The area around them was relatively flat and had it been July, they would be able to see for miles and miles. Still, despite the fact that the sun's rays were faint, Dan got a decent view. "Where's the fell from here?" he asked.

The other three pointed in the same direction. Liv said, "You would have been able to possibly see it a couple of hours ago in the distance." Just as she said that, a flickering glow of a light could be seen in the direction that they were looking. It caught all of them off guard, but Kirsti quickly went over to a wooden chest on the platform and pulled out a long thin telescope. She handed it to Pete, who was caught off guard because Kirsti had moved so fast. Kirsti also grabbed a pair of clamps and proceeded to the railing where she placed and then tightened the clamps a few inches apart. She took the telescope, loosened the clamps a bit and then placed the rectangular base of the spy apparatus under each clamp before tightening them up again. She pointed and focused the telescope in the direction of the fell. After briefly taking a look, she motioned to Dan to take a turn.

Dan looked through the eyepiece and watched the periodic light coming from the mountain. As this occurred every few minutes or so, he could see the fell's silhouette each time. It was both an eerie and beautiful sight all wrapped up in one package. He was hypnotized by it, but he backed away from the lens to let the others have a look. Each took a turn and then the light stopped.

Dan's first words were, "What in God's name was that?"

Kirsti said, "That, ahem, is what you're here for."

Dan asked, "Why aren't there more people coming to this area to investigate? This has to be a scientist's dream. Besides, if I was in your government, I'd want to know what the hell this was."

Kirsti answered, "First of all, you can't see this from everywhere. Even though it seems bright enough, the only people who seem to be able to see it are those who live around the fell. We can't explain why that is. Parts of the Russian side of the fell can see it too. Russian patrols periodically wander into our country illegally, on purpose or accidentally. This is why it appears that they know something's up too."

Pete added, "Dan, our job is to get the jump on the story, exploit it if we need to, or bury it if we have to. You have nothing to lose. You may end up with a great story and a nice new position. The worst is that you get nothing and you go home having quite an adventure."

Dan, with a stone-faced look, said in response, "Right. One that included getting shot at. At no extra cost."

The other three smiled and Liv pulled a flask out of her coat pocket. "Here. This will ease the tension a little. Polish brandy."

When the brandy made its way back to Dan, he paused, lifted the flask as if making a wedding toast. "Here's to whatever gets us through the night. And hopefully tomorrow."

15

THERE'S GOT TO BE A MORNING AFTER

Katri, along with an early rising Dan, had breakfast going. Coffee, bread, eggs and sausage were ready by the time everyone arrived at the table. Frans was outside gathering wood and checking on all of the vehicles. As he came in, a voice greeted him. "Here, take this in with you." Katri handed him a tray of bread and a pot of coffee to bring to the table. Eight were seated as Katri and Frans were shuffling about making sure everybody had everything they needed to enjoy the meal. It was seven o'clock and one could see it on most of the faces of the younger generation. Still, everyone was in high spirits and very talkative at the table.

When breakfast was over, all ten rose methodically from the table and helped clean their individual messes. Frans disappeared for a few minutes and then came back wearing his winter clothing. He said, "I'll warm up the half-track." The rest gathered up their belongings and within fifteen minutes, everyone said their goodbyes to Katri and proceeded to their vehicles. In a few moments, they began their excursion to the fell.

The ride to their next destination was full of bumps and icy turns, but relatively uneventful. They headed towards a little cluster of cabins just a few miles from the fell. The people living there had been friends of Frans and Katri for ages and were considered family. Their existence in the fell region went back many generations, they lived off the land and most spoke little to no English. How the friends came to possess the bodies was unclear to Dan.

It was still quite dark when the travelers stopped; several people came outside to greet them as they pulled in front of the middle cabin. They looked like dark shadowy creatures until they stepped into the headlights of the half-track.

A voice from these shadows called out to them. "Hei!" The first man who stepped forward to greet them was Eerikki Neikkinen. He was Frans' age and just as rugged. Frans referred to him as Erik when they spoke to one another. Several more people came out, both men and women, from the different cabins that were all within a stone's throw from each other. Most of them looked to be about Frans' age too, but there were a few closer to Dan's age here and there. He was introduced to everyone, but couldn't remember their names. Pete didn't know any of these people firsthand, but his cousins did. Dan didn't count the number, but he later estimated that there were ten or eleven of them.

Erik quickly got down to the serious business at hand. He politely spoke in English due to Dan being the only one who didn't speak Finnish. "Follow me." He led the way to the backwoods of the tiny settlement. There, he continued on for about a hundred yards to a small shed. He stopped in front of it and turned to face Dan and the others.

He said, "What you are going to see is alarming. All of my friends and family here have seen it and the memory still haunts them." He opened the doors and went into the already lit structure. A small generator, which provided the electricity for the shed, could be heard humming in the back. Erik showed them two wooden tables which were covered with canvas tarps. Without wasting any more time, he and Frans pulled the tarps off.

16

The two men revealed what looked like four badly burned bodies. Nobody spoke, not even a muffled gasp. The only ones seeing this for the first time were Dan, Pete and Liv. Dan moved closer to examine the horrible sight. He asked Erik, "May I?" Erik nodded. Dan gestured for Pete to come closer and said, "Take out your digital camera." Dan took out his own cell phone and began to film what he saw. What he was looking at left him speechless. He touched nothing. He couldn't yet bring himself to get that personal with them. Pete began taking photos.

Dan summoned the nerve to speak. He narrated what he thought he was seeing. "I'm identifying four separate entities twisted amongst each other. One looks like a giant dog, as Jaako had previously mentioned. It is twice the size of a Great Dane, but closely resembles a Doberman. Two of the others resemble only each other. They are definitely animals, of some sort, but they are different from the dog-like creature. They are roughly the same size as the first animal, but they each have horns. I think. The possible horns are curved like that of a goat, which gets rid of any notion that they are reindeer or elk. One of them appears to be missing a horn, which looks to be embedded in the body of the fourth victim."

The fourth body was even more intriguing and more mysterious than the other three. It was animal-like but yet it wasn't. Dan couldn't make out everything because this body had suffered the most damage and appeared to have two arms and two legs, but the ends of each limb were burned off. The face was almost human in nature, but it too had been badly damaged in what looked to have been close range fighting. His or her face showed evidence of once having a great deal of hair, leading Dan to believe that it was a he. What made the body difficult to describe as being human, was the hard leather appearance, more like animal hide than skin. The force that it took to drive the horn deep into its abdomen must have been incredible.

Dan asked Erik and Frans, "Can we turn this one over?" They agreed and Erik went to the back of the shed and brought back a long piece of lumber. He and Pete took one side of the board. Frans and Dan took the other side. With two men on each side of the table, they put the side of the wood under the left side of the body and together they pushed until they flipped the body on its side, careful not to disturb the stomach and horn. Dan went over to where Erik had gotten the wood and found a thin foot long piece. He went back to the table and used the stick to push away the creature's long hair and exposed the back of its neck where it wasn't burnt. Dan took off one of his gloves and carefully put a finger on the subject's neck. Frans, Erik and anyone else who could see, leaned in with great interest when he did this.

Dan was trying to get a better idea of what the skin actually looked like. He saw that it was leathery like the burnt skin, but it was more of a gray rather than the charcoal color caused by fire. When he moved away more of the hair, he could hear a gasp come from the crowd. Someone whispered loudly, "Tonttu." Dan turned slightly around to see that even though the shed was relatively small, half of the people were able to squeeze themselves near the doorway to see.

Based on the reading he had done while waiting for Pete and Jaako to pick him up at the airport, Dan knew that a tonttu was a gnome or elven creature associated with Joulupukki, the Finnish version of St. Nicholas. Depending on whose tale one wanted to believe, a tonttu could be good or evil. The crowd's reaction was based on a mark branded or tattooed in a magnificent shade of black with gold flecks, which made it stand out from the relatively dark gray skin coloring. The mark was a symbol or letter. Dan lifted his phone and took a close photo. He looked to see what he had and then turned around and showed the people nearest to him the picture. The people opened their mouths upon seeing the й.

Frans asked Dan if he had seen enough. Dan nodded and helped cover the bodies. He walked outside and asked what the mark meant. "Cyrillic," Erik said. Dan knew that Cyrillic was a writing system developed over a thousand years ago and was most commonly used in parts of Europe and Asia such as Turkey, Russia and several Slavic nations, but its use was dying out.

Dan asked, "What letter is on his neck?" Erik and Frans looked at each other to see who was going to answer.

Frans took the lead. "The best way to explain it is to say that it most closely resembles Russian Cyrillic, although it's been used by other countries too. It's an 'I', but it has been replaced by the letter J."

Dan put his hand outward as if to stop Frans. "So, it's a J. Why a J?" He looked at Frans and Erik, but he realized that all eyes were staring at him. "Wait a minute. Are you guys saying it means J for Joulupukki? As in the goat-man? As in the Finnish Santa?"

Nobody said a word. They didn't have to. Everyone was quite familiar with the legend except Dan, who only had a rudimentary knowledge of the legend. He was very uncomfortable; and felt as if everyone was in on a joke but him. He excused himself and made his way to the crowded doorway. The group of people there made an opening for him and he went outside. Pete followed him. When the two of them were away from everybody, Dan turned and said, "You need to explain everything to me, now. I know that there's more than you and the rest of your family aren't telling me. I'm not going anywhere else until somebody tells me something."

Pete looked down at his own feet and found the courage to answer him. "Okay. Everything Frans told you earlier was true, whether you want to believe it or not. He told you that they were tales, but they aren't. And he didn't tell you everything. He was trying to feel you out, to see what your reaction would be. You didn't flinch too much, so I think you're ready for the next chapter."

Dan interrupted him. "You mean to tell me that you withheld things from me? So, everyone else is in on this but me. Great."

Pete didn't have the words to defend himself or his family. All he could say was, "That's fair Dan. We held off telling you about everything, but we had a good reason. We didn't want you to think right off that we were crazy. I mean, come on, would you have believed me if I told you everything on the trip from the airport? We gave it to you in small doses, so that you wouldn't find the eventual truth so unbelievable. All of us here have been living with these stories for years, especially my grandparents and cousins."

Dan asked, "Why don't you tell me everything now? I'm ready."

Pete took a breath first. "Well, as I said, my grandfather's conversation about Thor, special powers and the fell are pretty much spot on. I don't know about the Thor stories exactly, but the strange power left behind is real. I don't know if it was caused by the destruction of a magic hammer or not. All I know is that there have been strange forces at work in this park for years and years. I'm going to tell you other things that you're going to find hard to process."

Dan posed an interrupting question. "Why don't the people around the fell just leave? I mean, if I lived here, I'd probably go. And don't tell me it's the same reason why people don't leave their homes if they're supposedly haunted. You know, because they have no place to go."

Pete interrupted him right back. "No. I'm not gonna say that, because that's not the reason. They don't leave because the man or being behind all of this activity around the fell protects them."

Dan was not expecting this. The only thing he could say was, "What?"

Pete continued. "He protects them. He takes care of them. I don't know for how long, but he's been doing this for a very long time, at least since the 1800s. This part of Finland has survived invasions, rebellions and even two world wars. We don't know where he came from and why he does this."

Pete paused to watch Dan's reaction and Dan asked, "What do you mean by taking care of them? Does he feed them, clothe them, plow their driveways?"

Pete didn't waiver from his explanations. "He takes care of them by making sure they have enough to survive the cruel winters up here. Every December, the people around the fell receive food and other items that help them. Dried meat, preserved fruit and vegetables, clothing and even metal tools anonymously appear at the doorstep of the settlers of this region." Pete waited to see Dan's reaction.

Dan continued with his tough approach. "The next thing you're going to say is that he brings candy and toys to the little ones." Pete just stared at him. "Oh, come on now. Don't even say it." Pete motioned to Dan with his finger to turn around. Dan didn't realize that all of Pete's family, Erik and several of the other people had quietly gathered to listen. Dan suddenly felt like he was in a Finnish version of *The Children of the Corn.*

Frans added to the conversation, "He does bring small things for the children so that they aren't left out. Many of us don't need the food and supplies anymore because we are self-sufficient, but we still receive a token something like socks or blankets, at the same time every year. I know what you're thinking. We're describing Santa Claus or Joulupukki. We are and we're not. Santa Claus is a fabrication handed down through the generations in many different countries. The first incarnate of the man was St. Nick or Nicholas. He was a real person who was extremely generous to people centuries ago in Turkey, but his memory has been commercialized by America and Europe. Here in Suomi, his home has been put in the city of Rovaniemi. That's fine for the children and tourists, but the real story lies here. And the story comes out of our region's desperation to survive and the kindness of a mysterious being. You can believe us or not believe us. But know this, each year in late December something strange and amazing happens for the few hundred homesteads around the fell in our country and Russia."

Dan looked at the faces of the people around him and sensed their agreement with Pete and Frans. At this point, everyone was around him as if he was being accused of something. The only thing he was being accused of was not being a believer. "Okay," he said reluctantly. "So, what do we do now?"

Pete was trying to figure out how to respond. What he was about to say to Dan could cause one or both of them ending up with a few contusions and abrasions. "Dan. You don't have to do anything. You are free to leave and go back to the U.S."

Dan responded to this with a resounding, "Come again?" He then looked around as if somebody might have a better answer, but none was forthcoming. "Are you messing with me?"

Pete stared at Dan with firm conviction. "You can go, but you can't leave until tomorrow night. By the time you make it back to New York, it should be at least three days from now. That will give us plenty of time."

This time, it was Dan's turn for firm conviction. "Plenty of time for what? What the hell is going on?"

Pete moved closer to Dan. "I'm sorry Dan, but I, uh, we needed to get you here from New York. Your service was greatly appreciated."

It was as if Dan was spewing lava. "What do you mean by my service? Are you saying that you used me?" Pete turned to everyone else and spoke to them in Finnish. The group calmly dispersed. Pete motioned to Dan to walk with him. "How did you use me? Why?" Pete and Dan walked out of voice range from the rest.

Pete turned and said, "Okay. Here it is plain and simple. I needed an excuse to stay here in Finland for an extended period of time. The only way that I was going to be able to do that and keep my news job was to tell Roger Harbinger that there was a story here." Dan wanted to interrupt but Pete held him off. "I know. I know. You're gonna say, 'But Pete, there is a story here.' Well, yes and no. Yes, there is a story. There's always been a story here. But no, there is no story for you. You need to go home."

"Why?" Dan asked.

Pete answered him quickly. "You have to go because it's probably going to get extremely dangerous around here and none of us would want that. Dan, all of these people you see around you have been highly trained or have lived here long enough to know what's ahead of them. This isn't your fight. I brought you here for a selfish reason."

"If you didn't want me to be involved, then why show me the bodies?" Dan asked. "You could have brought me here just as you did, had me drive around with you guys for a few days and then sent me packing without a story. Well, now there is a story."

Pete paused and decided to tone down his words. "No Dan, there isn't. There can't be. We showed you those bodies to get you to sympathize with us. We knew that with your investigative nature, you'd know that we were hiding something. Everybody here was against telling you, but I told them that you would smell that something was off. Now I know this is a lot to ask, but I need for you to go back to *The Mob* and tell Roger that there's nothing newsworthy here. I was supposed to accompany you back, but I should hopefully only be a day or two behind. My flight arrangements are already set."

Dan didn't know what to say. Pete continued. "Maybe you do have an actual purpose here. If you don't hear from me or my family, you need to communicate to one of your many contacts that there was a problem. You have the evidence on your phone as proof that something strange is going on here. Don't give them to Roger. Putting them in a newspaper would be a bad thing for all of the people here. We don't want you to post a story online or in print. As I just told you, I made up that scenario for you and Roger, just to get him to agree to send you."

Dan tried to digest everything that was just force fed to him, but it was too much to handle. He was also getting cold from standing outside for so long. He said, "Pete, you said nobody here wanted me to learn about all of this but you. They could have stopped you from allowing it to happen. There's only two of us against all of them."

Pete laughed. "They tried. Those snowmobiles didn't randomly disappear. They were taken by a few of the people here to slow us down. Or rather to slow you down. That SUV that we were in was not supposed to have broken down, especially where it did. Then like a bloodhound, you found the machines and we were back in business sooner than everyone had hoped."

Dan still felt that Pete was holding something back. He asked, "What about the Russians and all of the shooting? If you guys are so well trained, why would Arturo pop his head up like that and become a target?"

Pete shook his head and replied, "The shooting was not planned, of course, but it wasn't the Russians. It was us. It was friendly fire."

"Friendly fire? You shot your own cousin?" Dan asked. "Who did the shooting?"

Pete took out a walkie talkie, only it wasn't a walkie talkie but a satellite phone. It took Dan a moment to distinguish it from the two. "Come on in," Pete said over the phone.

"Who's coming in?" Dan asked.

Pete stood briefly silent before answering him. "Dan. I'm not actually a reporter. Well, on the surface I am. It's just a cover. I work for the FSIS, aka The Finnish Security Intelligence Service. Well actually, an offshoot of it. And I'm on loan to the CIA."

Dan angrily asked. "Really Pete? How far is this whole story going to go?"

Pete reached into his pocket and pulled out what appeared to be a small wallet. He flipped it open, revealing an ID and a badge. Then he pulled out a second one revealing yet another set of credentials.

He continued his story. "My job at *The Mob* affords me the freedom to take on cases every once in a while. When I go out on assignment, it's usually a fabrication by my government or yours. We make up a reason for me to go and the newspaper is none the wiser. That's why Roger is reluctant to send me out on big news items, because most times I come back with no news." Dan was stunned. He shook his head and was about to speak when Pete interrupted, "Joe Archer."

"Wait. What?" Dan asked.

Pete repeated, "Joe Archer. He's a mutual acquaintance of ours."

Dan was ready to take a knee. He asked, "Is he the one you just called?"

Pete replied with a simple, "No." A few sets of lights suddenly appeared on the narrow road in front of them. Nobody even heard the new group of people arrive.

Pete quickly tried to stop him, but Dan walked towards the lights yelling, "Archer! Archer!"

A few dark figures appeared in front of him. Dan had difficulty seeing because the lights on their stealthy machines were still lit. As the figures approached, one stood out. It was a man, rather large in size, with an incredible John Wayne-like walk. He bellowed, "Hello Dan. Good to see you again." The stranger took off his black ski mask and turned on a small flashlight, revealing the mystery. Dan's mouth opened a mile. It was Andy Warwick.

17

THERE'S A NEW SHERIFF IN TOWN

After Dan's initial reaction wore off a little, Andy began the conversation. "I'm Joe's secret contact. You know, the one he calls James Bond. I was on the plane with you to try to get a sense of who you were. I would have been on the next flight too, but I knew you made me."

Dan asked, "Made you?"

Andy said with a laugh, "Bob Vila. 'That was good, real good. I quickly looked it up on my phone when I could and realized that you knew that I was a phony. Right there and then I knew that we had the right man for the job."

"They're dumping me." Dan replied.

Andy responded, "No we're not. Not anymore. Pete isn't aware of everything that's recently been going on. We have been in contact with someone you know who has had to help us. We need for you to talk to that person right now." Andy reached into his pocket and pulled out his own satellite phone. After a few moments, he spoke into it.

"Hello? Yes. I made it to within three miles of our final destination. Yes. He's here." Andy held the phone out to Dan.

Dan bristled but still pressed the receiver to his ear. "This is Dan."

He heard a voice on the other end that was very familiar, but the ultimate shock of it turned his head inside out. An excited but serious sounding voice spoke to him, "Hello Danny!"

Dan looked at Andy and asked, "Grandma Rina?"

It turned out that Rina's corporation was heavily involved in supplying state of the art technology to the United States government, along with a few friendly nations, including Finland. Although for Rina to get involved in the day-to-day affairs of her businesses at this point in her life was unusual, she usually left that up to Dan's father Marcus. Finding out that her only grandson was in on this little escapade caused her to move to the head of the class of involvement.

"Hello, my favorite grandson," Rina continued. "When I heard that you were still mixed up in all of this, I knew that I had to give your spy friends everything they requested and more. Nothing is going to happen to my little boy." The over six feet tall Dan stood there and grinned. Rina would somehow always think of him as perpetually being twelve years old.

"Rina." He sometimes dropped the 'Grandma' part. "How and when did you know I was with these guys?"

Rina replied hesitantly, "I knew a couple of weeks ago. They told me not to say anything to you, until now." Dan couldn't believe that his grandmother knew before he did. She added, "I just wanted to hear your voice and know that you were safe. Now go have a good mission or whatever it is. Love you."

Dan laughed a bit. "Thanks Grandma. I love you too. Bye." Dan turned and faced Andy and Pete. "You mean to tell me that she knew I was going to be here even before I agreed on the assignment?" They both nodded. "You guys were really ahead of yourselves, weren't you? How could you have been so sure?"

Andy answered him. "We had no choice, because your family's business had developed some great equipment for us, but Rina and your grandfather were reluctant to send anything that was still in the demo stage. With you along, we felt that that would seal the deal."

In fact, the CIA and Andy's unnamed spy agency had purchased many items from Rina's business over the years and they had also bought a few hi-tech devices specifically for this mission. Dropping Dan's name into a conversation with Marcus and Rina, meant a few other experimental items were included free of charge. Andy needed

Dan to stay involved in order to justify receiving the extra goods.

"What kind of equipment?" Dan asked.

Andy said, "Well for one, you didn't hear us approach you on our snowmobiles until we turned our lights on. That's because they're muffled to a point where they're virtually noiseless. And these machines can switch over to electric power without skipping a beat. If we go electric, then we're even harder to detect on any listening devices. Our night vision helmets are more than just for seeing at night. First of all, looking through them is just like seeing things on a sunny day. They have a micro-computer installed in them that allows us to detect things and then it analyzes what we see or think we see. We can see things that are more than a foot underground or inside a wall. It also tells us distance, has radar, listening devices, communications devices and has an infrared laser pointer that is in sync with our weapons. The laser guides the bullets like much bigger lasers guide missiles. We look, we point, we shoot. It makes ground warfare easier."

Dan was having a hard time wrapping his brain around all the new information; he was in disbelief that his parents and grandparents were in the killing business. Andy noticed Dan's facial expressions. "Listen," Andy said. "I know what you're thinking. But your family doesn't deal in arms manufacturing. They make technology that is tied in with weapons, but technically they don't make any weapons. Our government wanted them to, but your grandmother said absolutely not. We have people who can alter your family's technology to fit our weaponry. We needed you here because they make awesome non-lethal products and some of them are not on the market yet. You were the ace in the hole. She sent us everything and then some, because you're here. I know you think we conned you and used you. Well, we did to an extent. If we don't find anything too unusual at the fell, then you go home without a story or you can write a fluff piece on beautiful Finnish women to justify to your boss your trip here. If we find something supernatural, then the story can't get out. You understand that, right?"

Dan felt that he was being threatened without Andy or Pete coming right out and saying it. All he could conjure up as a response was, "Got it." He did have a few questions of which he felt he was entitled to answers. "What happened to that cabin that was torched? Who did it? Was it you and your men?"

Andy smiled and yelled to his comrades who were standing near their snowmobiles. "Hey Washington and Torino! Come here for a minute!"

Two of the men walked over to Andy and stopped. He said loudly to them. "Take off your headgear." As they removed their helmets and then their ski masks, Dan realized that they were not men at all. Andy said, "We are an equal opportunity employer. You asked if it was my men. We have women too." Two serious-faced women stared intently at Dan. "Okay, you can go." They retreated back to the snowmobile gang.

Dan wasn't sure what Andy's purpose was with showing him the two women at that moment, so he asked again. "And the torched cabin?"

Andy answered, "That is an unknown. We'd like to blame the Russians, but they had no reason. And before you ask, no, we didn't light up that Russian patrol either. I think it's tied to the dead bodies, since they suffered a similar fate. Maybe the same people who burned these bodies, did the same to the cabin and to the patrol. I don't know if we'll ever really know."

Dan continued with his questions. "Since I'm obviously heavily involved, can you tell me everything you know about what's going on?"

Andy looked over at Pete and asked, "How much has he been told?"

Pete replied, "My grandfather told him all of the mythology stuff and we also let him know about the being who is the Protector of this area."

Frans had wandered over and interrupted the conversation. "We believe that the Protector is under attack. His very existence is in danger. You saw the tonttu body and the bodies of those other creatures. We think that a battle has begun over the power that is contained in the fell. The tonttu was a follower of Joulupukki. The other creatures are the enemy. Our job is to make sure that everything remains in balance. If the Protector is destroyed, who knows what kind of evil will be unleashed around the fell or for that matter, around the world."

Dan looked at Andy and Pete to elicit a response. Andy nodded, "We know what Frans knows. Our mission is to go in and tip the scales in favor of the Protector. We have been asked by the Finnish government to get involved. Our two governments have a mutual interest in keeping the Russians out of it, not because we can't use their help, but because we don't know what we will find at the fell. If the power of an ancient destroyed hammer of mythology is there, we don't want Russia to obtain it. We don't actually know who the Protector's enemies are, but whoever they may be, they seem to be a formidable opponent and may be responsible for the tonttu's death.

"The tonttus, I'm told, are the right-hand men of the Protector. Look, I don't necessarily believe in all of this mythology stuff, but something out of the ordinary is happening here. I've seen enough crap in my day to know that many things are possible. That's why my agency doesn't have a name. We investigate things that are not to be believed. We're just simply called by the name, The Agency. Even your pal Archer's CIA buddies don't know what we know. We tell them enough to get their help, give them permission to follow us around a little at home and overseas and then we leave them in the dark when we have to. Even the president isn't always sure what we do."

Dan asked, "What's the plan? Don't say that I'm not going with you, because I am. All of you have used me enough. I believe that I've earned the right to go."

Andy smiled and said calmly, "I've already said that you're going. But you need to know this. Everyone around you is trained to go into the heat of battle. Even many of the settlers here have been trained, to an extent, by the Finnish version of the CIA to protect the secret of the fell. If you slip up, it could cost you your life or the life of somebody in the group. That's why you need to stay out of the line of fire, if there is any fire. Can you handle a weapon?" Dan nodded yes. Andy continued, "Good. Go over to my team and get the necessary guns and gear for our little escapade. We leave in an hour."

After Dan was out of earshot, Andy looked at Pete and said, "First chance you get, make sure he's disabled so that he can't travel the full excursion with the group. We don't need Bambi messing things up for us. Be sure to make it look like an accident. And for God's sakes don't kill him. We need his family to continue providing us with all of those pretty gifts they build."

Pete nodded nervously in agreement. The thought of him having to hurt Dan in order to protect him chilled him to the bone. He hoped that fate would somehow intervene and he would never get the chance to comply with Andy's orders.

Dan walked quickly over to the anonymous agency members and received his equipment and a rundown on how the advanced electronics of his helmet worked. He was also told what their mission was going to be. It was rather simple. The parade of people on snowmobiles would move stealthily towards the fell. They would engage any hostile forces along the way. Upon reaching the fell, they would aid the Protector in any way necessary. They would then leave when the mission had been accomplished.

To Dan, this was too simple to be true. First of all, if supernatural forces were at work, could a crew of thirty or so humans on snowmobiles help? Secondly, wilderness St. Nick appeared to have his own powers and thirdly, the power of Thor's broken hammer, if it even existed, could easily disintegrate all of them. This power in the wrong hands could easily fend off Andy's little invasion force, especially those four, maybe five people who were up in age. Dan thought about the dead bodies and the sizes of a couple of the victims. Whatever killed them was, in its own right, a mighty adversary.

Dan stood by himself immersed in his thoughts while everyone around him prepared for war. More questions remained unanswered. Why weren't the Finnish and American governments more involved? Both countries had sent representatives that were comprised of this posse on hi-tech horseback. Why didn't they just send in an army with air support and just lay waste to the perceived enemy? These questions burned inside his gut to the point where as Pete was walking by, Dan grabbed his arm, "Talk. Now."

Pete protested due to the urgency to get ready, but he eventually relented and agreed to let Dan say what was on his mind. Dan asked, "Am I missing something? If these beings are supernatural, then we can't possibly affect the outcome between good and evil."

Pete had come clean with almost everything, but he was still hiding a big piece of the puzzle. He decided to fill in the last blank. "Listen Dan. None of us believe that we can affect the overall outcome of a battle between powerful beings. If our guy wins, then we turn around and go home. If our guy loses, then we do what we can against the other. However, we believe the Protector will win. Andy and both of our governments want to make sure that the Russians, if they show up, don't make off with anything of super power value in the ensuing chaos. We're going to be there in case they're going to be there. And we believe that they are in the area already. Joulupukki is powerful, but he probably has limits. If he didn't, then this predicament wouldn't exist."

Dan asked, "How can a group that includes a few up in age people be effective against anyone, supernatural or not?"

Pete said, "They probably can't be that effective. They're coming for two reasons. The first is that they live here and demanded to be involved.

They were able to make demands because they were refusing to provide any info to us until we agreed. The second reason is that we don't know if their protector will be responsive to us strangers coming near the fell by ourselves. Having the settlers with us will hopefully show him that we are not his enemy."

Dan and Pete's conversation was interrupted by Andy, "Everyone get on your snowmobiles."

They still had more than a half hour until their actual departure time, but Andy had received word through a surveillance drone that Russians were spotted near the fell. Time to go. After putting on their headgear, everyone started their electric machines. Kirsti walked by Dan and pressed a button on his helmet and then kept walking to her own mount. All of a sudden, darkness turned into daytime as the night vision power kicked into gear. He could read words and numbers that were superimposed onto the inside of his helmet's face shield. As he turned his head from side to side, he was informed of the distance of objects he looked at. Mikko pressed another button on Dan's helmet as he walked by and Dan could hear a voice speaking to him.

Mikko said, "Dan, don't forget, you can talk to your helmet and ask it questions. Be sure to tell it to sync with your voice. You then need to be sure that your weapons are also connected."

Dan remembered most of the very brief mini-lesson that he was given on the workings of his equipment. His helmet, guns and snowmobile were electronically tied to each other. He was amazed that his grandparents' company made all of this possible. Their organization was truly a deep tech enterprise. In his travels, he had seen similar technology, but none this advanced. He waited until the caravan in front of him moved until he followed suit. There were thirty-four of them. Most were in front of him as they moved along, with six in back. When the trail got wider, two riders on each side of him magically appeared. He was being shielded and he knew it.

18

HELL IS WAR

It was still two hours before the midday sunrise would occur. Their travel was reasonably fast with no glitches. As Dan approached, the fell appeared daunting. Although easily seen through his helmet shield, surrounding the fell was a strange haze. He began to recklessly think that their little soirée would continue to move along quite nicely with no speed bumps. According to Dan's helmet, they were less than a mile away. Trying to figure out which rider was Kirsti, he used the magnification feature of his face shield to zoom in on the rider's way in front of him. He hadn't been aware that this technology was part of the helmet's package. He took a chance and said, "Zoom in fifty percent." The face shield proceeded to comply with his order instantaneously, which shocked him to the point where he shifted back in his seat, catching the attention of his armed babysitters on both sides.

One of the agents proceeded to ask him, "Everything okay Mr. Becket?"

Dan never got the chance to answer him. A bright flash shot out in front of them along with a deafening humming sound. Every rider was thrown from their machine. Within an instant, Dan found himself not only off of his snowmobile, but also off of the road entirely. He was too dazed to have any idea of what had just happened. He remembered later, that he had looked up and saw people dangling in trees.

At this point, he couldn't comprehend the situation. All he could do was crawl. He inched his way slowly back onto the narrow road. Along the way, he saw people everywhere. Some were moving, most were still. Everyone's protective clothing seemed to be smoking. He also saw burned-out snowmobiles. There were sparks flying and people in pain, but he could hear virtually nothing, except for a very loud vibrating ringing in his ears. Despite being disoriented, he had been able to pull his body over a snowbank and back to the part of the road he was on before the mysterious catastrophe had occurred.

He looked around for people he recognized, but no one was at the same spot they were moments before. Dan was finally able to sit up, but he wasn't able to stand quite yet. As he tried to raise his head, his neck felt like he had been dragged behind one of the snowmobiles. His forehead felt like it was about to split open. It was difficult to focus his eyes.

Five minutes later, Dan was able to see a little more clearly. His helmet's electronics were still functioning and he attempted to get up and walk, no easy task, but after several attempts, his shaking legs finally gained traction and allowed him to stand. His back was in knots, but he limped to the people closest to him. He didn't recognize them, but he figured they were either settlers or part of Andy's crew. Some were breathing and others appeared to be dead. Dan looked for Pete, the four cousins, Frans and Liv. He saw a person hanging from the bottom limb of a tree that was hanging over the road. The figure was that of a female. She appeared lifeless, but he reached for her arm, which was hanging down within his grasp. Pulling, Dan was able to dislodge her from the tree, only to have her land hard on top of him.

Despite all of this rough handling, the woman remained unmoving. Dan positioned her on her back and removed her helmet. As he pulled her ski mask off, his jaw froze in terror. It was Kirsti. Her face already looked gray from a lack of oxygen. He leaned over her, took off his helmet, and started to perform mouth to mouth resuscitation. Although the air so cold, his face was sticking to hers but he didn't stop from trying to save her life. His eyes began to tear up as he began to realize that his chances of saving her were lessening as the seconds rolled by.

With all of the winter clothing along with a protective chest shield on her, Dan was having difficulty determining whether her heart had stopped. Because of her appearance, he took a chance and assumed it had. His breaths were soon joined by CPR compressions. Given his current state of mind, he had no idea if he was even doing it right. His fried brain wouldn't let him keep an accurate count of compressions and he was unsure if his breaths were too weak or too strong. He removed Kirsti's shield in order to make his compressions more effective.

He was suddenly aware of others beginning to stir all around him, but he continued to tend to the task at hand. He couldn't stop to see who was alive. His mind kept counting breaths and compressions, breaths then compressions. He was exhausted and it seemed as if he was going at it full steam for ten minutes or so. In actuality, it had only been about a minute. He yelled out, "Come on Kirsti! Come back to us!" Kirsti was not cooperating. Her limp, motionless body appeared to accept the ultimate eventuality of all human beings, but Dan refused to accept this. As he worked hard, he realized that several people had encircled them. He sensed that they were members of her family given their close proximity to the two of them.

Desperation was quickly settling in for Dan. He hardly knew this young woman, but he felt that he had made some kind of connection with her. He felt the extreme grief in the breathing and sounds of the people around him, which only pushed him harder to succeed. At this moment, Dan had no concept of time. Suddenly he stopped, as if he had given up the fight and was angry at death for stealing her. Dan surprised himself and everyone when he put his two fists together and pounded her chest with one powerful punch. He screamed, "Kirsti!"

No one had time to react to Dan's exhibition of hopelessness. As soon as his hands made contact with her, Kirsti let out a gasping breath that knocked some of her kneeling family members on their backsides. A CPR manual might not have condoned his technique, he later thought, but the proof was in the result. Dan had saved Kirsti's life.

She was coughing and struggling to breathe, but she was alive. As Pete, Jaako and Aleksi welcomed her back to the world of the living, Dan rolled from his knees to his left side from sheer energy depletion. All he could muster was, "Oh thank God." He stared at her for a few minutes before rising to his knees again. He kept watch to see if Kirsti would continue to breathe until his thoughts strayed to the other members of his party. He raised his head and took inventory of who was present. He didn't see Andy, Arturo, Liv, Frans, Mikko or Erik. He saw blurry images of people moving in the distance, but he had no idea who they could be.

Dan asked the group around him, "Where are the others? Arturo, Liv, Mikko, your grandfather?" Jaako and Aleksi slowly stood and looked towards the moving figures. Dan added, "And Andy? And, uh Erik?" He clumsily rose to his feet and leaned over Kirsti. He softly spoke to her. "How are you feeling, young lady?"

She weakly answered, "Like someone who was just kicked in the chest." She managed a faint grin. Even though she was unconscious during her ordeal, she sensed that Dan was somehow responsible for her rising from the unliving.

She reached her hand out to him and he reciprocated. "I have to go look for the others," he told her. "But I'll be back to check on you." Kirsti gave him a slight smile. Dan called out, "We need to find the others. Let's spread out and see if anyone needs help."

Aleksi stayed with Kirsti as the others fanned out to look for survivors. Along the way, people were stumbling around doing the same thing as Dan, looking for signs of life. He couldn't believe what he was seeing. People were strewn about all over the snow. Some were on the road. Others were thrown into the woods. Still others were thrown with so much force that they had been launched into the air. One body had been impaled by a short, broken branch and was hanging flush against a pine tree. Dan doubted that he or she survived.

Pete found Liv who cried, "Over here!" She had been thrown so far that she was not visible from the road. Her yells for help were what got Pete's attention. He slid down a snow bank to reach her. From the way she was holding her arm, he guessed that her left shoulder was either broken or dislocated. He yelled for more assistance and two people came to help. One of the men he didn't recognize. The other was a more welcome sight, his cousin Arturo, who had been tossed not far from Liv. The three men gently lifted Liv up and moved her towards the road. Although they stumbled a few times, they were able to get her to more solid ground.

Next on the list of people from Dan's circle of acquaintances was Frans, who was found on a snowbank a few feet from the road. His face was bloodied. His helmet was shattered with pieces lodged in his forehead, cheeks and chin. He was conscious, but he couldn't move. He complained of extreme back pain and he couldn't feel his legs. It was determined by Agent Washington, one of Andy's crew, that Frans' spine was most likely broken.

Agent Washington was trying to reach any of the U.S. agents on her helmet radio, but it appeared that something was either blocking the transmission or had fried much of the communication equipment. She began shouting orders to anyone who was standing. "Bring any survivors to my position! We need to regroup and determine our next move!" People slowly but steadily responded to her commands. Within ten minutes, twenty-five of the original thirty-four were in a group together on the road.

Not accounted for were Andy, Mikko, Erik and Torino. Five others, who Dan was not familiar with, were also missing. Dan yelled to Washington, "There's a person stuck to a tree." Since most of the women that were in the original thirty-four were present, Dan guessed that the body was that of a male, given the size and frame. Washington pointed to Dan, Pete, Jaako and two others to try to retrieve the body.

They made their way to the tree and Jaako and another man volunteered to climb it and bring him down. They both scaled the pine tree carefully, but with a decent amount of speed. Upon reaching him, they paused due to the nature of the situation. The man still had his helmet on and he had been flung against the tree, back-first. A broken but solid branch was protruding from his abdomen. In order to get him down, they would have to pull him off of the limb. Jaako reached under the man's helmet and felt his neck. "He's dead. Let's just carefully slide him off and bring him down." With some difficulty, they removed him from the branch. By this time, Dan and Pete had climbed to just below them and grabbed the man as he was being lowered. The man was not tall, but he was heavy. That fit the description of at least a half dozen of the males in the group. Dan and Pete grabbed him under his arms and lowered him even further to the still unknown man below.

Soon everyone was back on the ground. Jaako, whose helmet was off, took out a small flashlight to see if it worked. He was surprised that it did. Even though there was still daylight left, it was dark in the forest where they were. Laying the man down, Pete removed the man's mostly intact helmet. Pete, Jaako and Dan all had the same look of disbelief on their faces. They all said, "Erik."

It was Erik, Frans' close friend. He had been near the front of the pack of snowmobiles, which took the brunt of the shockwave. The force of it was so powerful, that the people in the lead were thrown the furthest. Many of them were still not able to stand or were missing. Such was the case for Andy, Mikko and Agent Torino. They were not among the dead or injured.

Agent Washington was able to account for thirty of the thirty-four people. The count was twenty-eight alive, although several were seriously injured, two had died and four were missing. Besides Erik, the other fatality was an American agent from Andy's group named Kirk Shipley. Washington said, "Those without severe injuries, look for any equipment still working or damaged. Then group them according to the type of equipment. Start the piles over there." She motioned to the middle of the path they were on. "Check all of the snowmobiles and determine if any are still usable."

Helmets, weapons, gloves and pieces of snowmobiles were gathered and put in big piles. Ten men then went to find the snowmobiles, which were scattered everywhere. Most were on their sides and some were no longer on the road. Washington and four others went through the pile of items and removed those that were no longer of any use. Most of the weapons were relatively intact. Many of the helmets could still be worn, but at least half of them no longer had working electronics. The force that hit them seemed to either fry or put a great deal of stress on the helmets' radar, night vision or computer capabilities.

Eventually, fourteen snowmobiles that were still able to start were brought to the group. All of the others were either too banged up or had their electrical systems shorted out by the still unknown force. Every machine had suffered some sort of damage, but these fourteen were still road-worthy.

Agent Washington said, "Anyone with mechanical or electrical knowledge, inspect the snowmobiles."

Washington attempted to communicate with Andy, but was unable to do so. She had tried contacting her superiors in Washington, D.C., but likewise was unable to reach them. Her satellite phone appeared to be in working order, but it couldn't make a connection with anyone in the government. Because of the super-secret nature of her mission, they would probably be of no immediate help. She was instructed not to contact the Finnish government for the same reason. They were basically on their own to find a solution. The matter that was most pressing was getting the injured medical assistance and respectfully transporting the deceased.

With only fourteen snowmobiles and thirty bodies to transport, both living and dead, the group was desperate for a solution. Dan went over to Washington and said, "I've got an idea. May I use your satellite phone?" Dan paused a bit to try to remember the number he wanted to call. Dan dialed and after several rings, he spoke. "Hello Grandma Rina, this is Danny. I need your help."

Dan explained his group's predicament. Rina didn't ask any questions about the how's and why's of the mission. She knew quite a bit already due to her company supplying the hi-tech for them. Dan asked her, "Is there any way your company could manage a rescue mission? Wait, hold on a second. I'll put Agent Washington on the phone. Thanks Rina. Love you."

Washington took the phone. Rina needed to know their coordinates in order to send help. The phone Washington was using could provide that information. The helmets they had been wearing could do the same, if they were functioning properly. Washington relayed the necessary data and hung up the phone. She looked at Dan and said, "It will probably take hours. We may not have that much time. We need to dig shelters in the snow, light some fires and look for Andy and the rest of the missing."

The fifteen able-bodied members of the group broke up into two parties. One group went to dig shelters, the other lit fires and brought the injured close to the warmth of the flames. Washington and Pete discussed their next move. "We need to search for my team," Washington said. "I'm not going to put any of this on you, Pete. You can stay here with your family and friends. I'll take the remainder of my guys and head towards the fell."

Pete stared intently at Washington. He was both amazed and confused at her comments. "Why would you think that we would let you go in with just a few of you," he asked. "Dan and my cousins are going with you. I'll leave Arturo with my grandfather and you leave at least one of your agents with your wounded." Washington, realizing that her protests were useless, reluctantly agreed. With most of the settlers being injured and old enough to be grandparents, it was agreed that all but two of them should stay behind.

After the wounded had been gathered in one place, the equipment collected, and primitive snow shelters built, a total of twelve people were seated in snowmobiles. The group had lost nearly two hour's worth of time, and were anxious to proceed. Washington and Pete took the lead, followed by Dan, Jaako, Aleksi and seven others. The seven others were American and Finnish agents, along with two settlers. The settlers were crucial to the group because they could be used as a hall pass to get to their Protector.

The distance to the base of the fell was rather short, but soon Washington yelled, "Stop!" She dismounted, turned on a flashlight and motioned for everyone else to do the same. After they had all gathered around her, she posed a question. "Anyone else notice anything really peculiar?" She answered her own question almost immediately. "There's no evidence that Agent Warwick and the others went through here. There are no snowmobile tracks."

Pete and Jaako scanned the immediate area with their flashlights and found no trace of the missing four. Everyone stood in silence, each trying their best to understand the situation. Dan stood motionless as he processed everything. He thought back to when he stood up after the energy blast.

He approached Washington and Pete. Dan said, "Hey. That blast of energy and sound really devastated not only us, but also the terrain around us. Machines and people were thrown. Trees were broken and snow banks were leveled. Is it possible that the snow and ground beneath us could have been moved or altered in some way?"

Washington knew exactly what he was talking about. The path they were traveling was narrow with areas bordered by small hills that extended nearly straight up around them. The hills were laden with mounds of untouched snow and possibly loose stone. The force of the energy could have easily loosened anything at the top of these hills. Andy and the other three and their machines could have been not only thrown off the road, but also buried in an avalanche of snow, ice and rock.

Washington got on her machine and everyone else followed her lead. She spun her snowmobile around and spoke with everyone whose helmet radios were functioning. "Let's go forward a bit and look to see if we can spot anything unusual."

Dan said in a very low voice, "Everything about this whole situation is unusual."

Washington then said, "Point your helmets, if they're functioning, down to the ground. They can detect things a foot or so beneath the surface. We won't necessarily know what they are, but we can determine if they're manmade or not, or maybe even human."

The group drove slowly in three staggered lines. They were about a hundred yards away from their injured comrades when Aleksi got a hit registered in his helmet. He yelled out, "I got something!" He instinctively first said it in Finnish, but the non-natives figured out what he was trying to say. Everyone came to a sudden stop and those whose helmets were working properly, pointed their faces down towards Aleksi's spot on the ground. A few of them picked up different signals, but after a few minutes, they were able to narrow their search to a ten-by-ten area.

Several of the group got off of their machines and grabbed something to dig with. Some had small shovels that had managed to stay clipped to their snowmobiles through their earlier ordeal.

Others whose helmets were not functioning electronically, removed their visors and used them as mini shovels. Still others grabbed knives and started chopping away. Two of the group backed up their machines and pointed their headlights in the direction of the diggers. They proceeded to move the other snowmobiles in a circle around the other ten.

The sounds of the activity got noticed by some of the other sixteen members left behind. A couple of them mounted the two remaining working snowmobiles and headed in the direction of the noises. All of a sudden, bright lights and a shaking ground disturbed all twenty-eight group members. The two on the snowmobiles stopped about twenty yards from Dan and his group because the snow and ground around them seemed to shift abruptly. They watched in horror as the snow that Dan, Pete and the rest had been shoveling started to sink beneath them. They didn't move so as to not disturb the ground any further.

The cause of this mini earthquake was unknown until three large but stealthy helicopters flew above them. Two of them seemed to be the size of U.S. Army Chinooks, but they were virtually noiseless until they appeared over everyone on the ground. Dan knew that they had to be the secret products of one of his family's aerospace companies sent by Grandma Rina to rescue the wounded and confiscate all of the spy weaponry that was no longer being used.

They were a welcome sight. Because of their size, however, they couldn't land. The rescue and salvage mission would have to be done the old fashion way. Baskets would have to be lowered to pick up the dead, wounded and light equipment. Strong cables would have to be used to lift any unused snowmobiles.

Paratrooper-like individuals were the first to be lowered in order to tend to the wounded and to search for missing equipment. Some of them had scanning equipment to sweep the area and secure any top-secret equipment that hadn't already been placed in a pile by the survivors. While all of this was going on, everyone seemed to forget a dire situation that was still developing, everyone but Dan's group.

The shifting of the snow was a by-product of the sheer enormity and power of the helicopters. Washington, Dan, Pete and the rest of their little group were trying to get a foothold without disturbing the already unstable snow beneath them. The two individuals who rode out to investigate Aleksi's discovery, could only stare helplessly as the white ground continued to move. Then, in an instant, they were gone.

19

GONE BUT NOT FORGOTTEN

Dan and the rest of his entourage dropped into the unknown. Humans, machines and the rest of the equipment plummeted uncontrollably along with snow from ground level in tow. It seemed to Dan like it was in slow motion, but in reality, it happened quickly. Their downward trip took about three seconds to complete. The snow beneath them had cushioned their fall. The snow that followed buried them. Ice was in the mix, but a miracle of fate saved all of them from getting badly hurt. A few of them moaned, but overall, everyone was spared any serious injury.

Meanwhile, the group on the surface was in a state of despair. They did nothing, right after it happened. After the initial shock wore off, they got the attention of the rather busy paratrooper unit and explained the desperate situation to them. At the same time, Dan and company were attempting to dig themselves out of their predicament.

All were in one piece and when they were able to stand, they realized that they had fallen into a tunnel of some sort.

Washington said, "Everyone gather up any equipment you can find."

The snowmobiles had remained rather intact, but all of them were too buried to be useful. After everyone was accounted for, they assessed their dilemma. Each person was still wearing a helmet and all had at least one weapon at their disposal. Because not everyone's helmet was functioning properly, Washington shined a bright light in what she believed was the direction they had been traveling. A dark but wide rock-lined tunnel showed itself. She pointed the light upwards to show that the sudden hole that they had dropped from had filled itself in with more snow and ice. No one from above would know where they were, she thought.

She said to the group, "If everyone is ready and able to move out, I suggest we proceed in the same direction we were traveling. It doesn't look like we can go anywhere else."

Without any major conversations, the frozen dozen moved in two close groups of six. They knew they had to either be right under the fell or close to it. The mystery was soon solved.

In front of them emerged several shadowy figures, seven to be exact. This caused the twelve to stop and point their weapons. Washington, Pete and Jaako shined their flashlights at the oncoming silhouettes. They kept coming and the group moved in a defensive fashion until someone from the intruders yelled, "Don't shoot at us!"

Dan, Pete and Washington raised their right hands up to signify to the other nine to refrain from firing, at least for the moment. Dan and Pete both thought that they were Russians until they came within twenty feet. One of the shadows yelled, "Turn out those lights! They hurt our eyes!"

Out went the flashlights and the seven figures moved closer until they were less than ten feet away. Jaako and Aleksi murmured in unison. "Tonttu." Dan stared curiously at the newcomers until he realized that they looked similar to at least one of the scorched bodies that he had seen earlier.

They were shorter than all of the men in the group, but they didn't look it. Their bodies were muscular with skin that looked leather-hard. The clothing they wore did not appear to belong in the twentieth or twenty-first centuries. As a matter of fact, in Dan's mind, they belonged with Robin Hood and his Merry Men. Their clothing was somewhat drab, but well fitting. They didn't wear headgear and the weapons that they wielded were not anything that Dan and the rest had ever seen. They resembled lances with strange trigger assemblies.

The one who had yelled not to shoot appeared to be the leader. The others walked near him on both sides, but back about a step. Washington, Pete, Aleksi, Jaako and Dan stood in front of their own group. As the two groups sized each other up, the leader of the tonttus started speaking in a language that appeared to be a combination of Finnish, Asian and Martian. Pete made out a few of the words, except for the not-of-this-earth lingo and spoke back to him in a combination of Finnish and English.

The stranger gave what appeared to be a grin and asked mostly in English, "All of you can speak Anglo, yes?" Dan and the rest nodded. "Good. I am Balinn and these are some of my assistants. We are part of the Protector's security force."

Dan whispered to Pete, "This is an army unit. What does this Protector guy need with an army?"

Balinn continued. "You have fallen into a tunnel beneath the Protector's domain. I could ask you what you are doing here, but all of us already know the answer. We have been watching you for days."

Washington interrupted, "We are looking for part of our team. Have you seen them?"

Just as Balinn was about to respond, a flare-like stream of fire burst from a dark interconnecting tunnel and knocked two of his assistants to the ground. They were on fire, but Dan, Washington and Jaako quickly covered them with snow to lessen the damage. Pete and Aleksi knocked Balinn down to protect him and everyone else fell to the ground with their weapons pointing towards the threat. Because of the single blast, everyone assumed it was a lone assassin.

Soon, they all started firing their weapons in the direction of the flare burst. Balinn and his associates fired weapons that expelled flames similar to the attacker's. Fireballs left Balinn's sidearm in a steady stream. Soon, the entire area of the two tunnels seemed to ignite in a hellish nightmare. Flames flowed from the attacker's part of the tunnel. Balinn and company fired feverishly into the darkness.

Washington and her followers fired their vastly different but sophisticated weaponry into the unknown as well. The stone sides of the tunnels had erupted in liquid fire. They appeared to be burning, as if made out of wood. The battle lasted ten minutes. It ended when a loud and powerful force from a side tunnel had knocked every one of the combatants to the ground. Dan and his companions knew this feeling well. It was the same kind of force that had decimated their original group of thirty-four.

After the impact of the strange force, Balinn and his sidekicks, including the two scorched fellows, stood up. The twelve soon followed suit. The force was not as powerful as the one that attacked the thirty-four, perhaps due to it coming from the side tunnel. The two groups stood and waited to see what was to happen next.

A lone figure came out of the tunnel. He, she or it was relatively tall, taller than everyone of the twelve. As the creature came closer, it appeared to be wounded. Its gait was more of a limp and two broken bone-like fixtures protruded from the top of its head. One was similar to that of a ram. The other was more like a stump, likely created from a previous battle or two. Smoke surrounded its entire body.

One of Balinn's men spoke the name, "Joulupukki."

As the strange outline came closer, everyone pointed their weapons. It continued towards them, showing no fear. Members of the twelve turned on their flashlights and the creature was fully illuminated. It continued closer until coming to a stop within ten feet of them. Its clothes were almost non-existent, having been partially burned off in the battle. It seemingly stared at all nineteen of them individually at least once.

After a few moments, it spoke. "I am Joulupukki, the great Joulupukki."

The words were a combination of different Scandinavian languages. Pete and his cousins were able to translate. Dan was confused. He thought the real Joulupukki was a benevolent person as in the Protector. This creature looked half animal in appearance.

Dan turned to Pete and relayed his bewilderment. Pete quickly explained, "In early myths, Joulupukki was a powerful being who could be both benevolent and dangerous. It appears this goat guy is the real Joulupukki. Looks like we're all confused as to who's who. We even screwed up on who the tonttus follow."

Balinn added to the history lesson. "He became obsessed with power when he discovered a piece of Thor's hammer. The hammer had exploded into many pieces centuries before. The Protector also came into possession of many of the pieces. He traveled through Scandinavia to obtain them, but Joulipukki did the same. They fought many battles over these. The Protector readied himself for battle by fusing his pieces together. I am sure you saw the glowing lights."

Joulipukki stood still while listening to their bio of him, as if he was enjoying his notoriety. He soon tired of this and raised what appeared to be a broken staff. He yelled in Finnish, "Stop! Enough of this!" Dan didn't understand the words, but he got the idea. Joulupukki continued, "I am done with all of you!"

Before Joulupukki could do anything, a voice from further down the tunnel could be heard but not understood by the twelve. Joulupukki turned around and headed towards the sound. He raised his staff, but it was too late. Before he could do anything, a flash of light appeared so brightly that it momentarily blinded all nineteen of the spectators. Joulupukki was turned into a bonfire. Within seconds, Dan and the other eighteen spectators came to their senses.

They all turned their weapons towards the creature in unison. As if it had been coordinated in advance, they fired at him in non-stop fashion. He turned his attention to the nineteen and fired back at them. The staff-like weapon he used looked as if to have rock crystals loosely attached to the top of it. Their weapons had some effect on him, but he continued to attack them despite him being a flaming mess.

Another bright flash came from the tunnel. This time, the horned blow torch dissolved into fiery dust particles. Realizing that the blast must have come from the Protector, Dan weakly asked Balinn, "Exactly how was the Protector able to just destroy this goat?"

Balinn replied proudly, "The Protector had more pieces. The Protector not only had more of the pieces of the hammer, but he had also put them together to create a partially completed weapon, which made him even more powerful than his goat-man adversary. Joulupukki, on the other hand, did no such thing. He merely carried the pieces that he had collected in a crude satchel on his body with the biggest pieces being crudely attached to a staff. It was a powerful weapon, but not powerful enough to match the force of the Protector."

Joulupukki had gathered what he thought would be enough to win the war. He was wrong. He led his horned followers and dog-like creatures in battle against the Protector several times. This resulted in the previously four charred bodies and was also the force that killed and injured members of the thirty-four.

At this point, all of the tonttus but Balinn were sifting through the obliterated remains of the aggressor. As they found a piece of the hammer that had been on Joulupukki's staff, they celebrated quietly. When they found all of the pieces, they fell in line behind Balinn.

Dan was about to speak when a large shadow with a hammer-like tool in his left hand appeared. The individual was at least six and a half feet in height and appeared to be bulky, but not obese. The twelve stood awestruck, but the seven tonttu did not. They merely stepped out of the way to let the large being pass. As he came into view, he stopped and surveyed the situation. He did not utter a word. He looked at Balinn as if to say something telepathically, then he disappeared into the darkness of the tunnel.

Balinn turned to the twelve and said, "You will come with us."

Without protest, Dan and the others obeyed. They were in no position to refuse. The walk was relatively brief and led them to an underground village of sorts. The twelve saw other tonttus moving about. The tonttus appeared to ignore them as they entered a large hall.

Balinn turned and said, "Come into this room with me." After they followed, they were stunned by what they saw. Sitting were Agent Torino, Mikko and a Finnish agent known as Eurlickson. Everyone laughed and hugged each other before realizing that Agent Andy Warwick was not with them.

Washington and Dan said at the same time, "Where's Andy?"

Torino quickly responded, "He's alive. Don't worry. Come with me."

She led Dan, Pete and Washington down a narrow hallway to a rather large room. The rest of the twelve did not follow. Andy was sitting in a chair being tended to by a tonttu woman. At least Dan thought she was female. Andy looked very alive, but very much in pain. He greeted them as if he was arriving late to a bar where they were drinking. "Hey gang! Where you been?" They looked at him, unsure as to the severity of his wounds. Realizing their concern, Andy said, "Don't worry. That Joulu guy stuck me in my side with that staff of his. I went down but I'm not out."

Dan took a step back as the rest of the twelve came in to meet with Andy. He stood there in silence until he felt a presence behind him coming out of the shadows. He turned abruptly to see the Protector. The being stepped into the light to reveal his full features. He seemed even larger than before, but he took on a more human quality because he wasn't killing anyone at the moment. He had a brownish gray beard that was full but not extremely long. Even though he no longer had the hammer in his large hands, he looked like he could pick someone up by their nose and throw them over a house. No words were spoken between them until the Protector said in understandable English, "You are both amazed and confused by me. I understand."

Dan tried to choose his words carefully, but all he could conjure up was, "It's not every day that I come face to face with Santa Claus." He immediately felt both ashamed and stupid after saying that.

The Protector paused and then laughed. "Santa Claus. That's all you can come up with?" He continued on. "I can feel the many questions that you have in your thoughts. I will answer them before you can say them. Yes. I am a Protector of the people living around this fell. It has been my home for centuries and they are like children to me. The tonttus are family. They are extremely loyal to me as I am to them. I could extend my influence further out into the world, but that is not my wish; people would start worshiping me because of all of the power and the longevity of life that the pieces of the hammer bring. Thor got caught up in all of that and look what happened, he was defeated and the hammer was broken into many pieces. Why he was given the hammer in the first place by a higher power is beyond my understanding. It surely was not for the purpose of him being thought of as a deity. Only God deserves that honor."

Dan asked, "Why was I brought into all of this? Why are you speaking only to me now?"

The Protector responded after a short pause. "I don't know the answer to your first question.

Perhaps your comrades can provide you with the information you seek. They may have seen your worth and trusted you." The Protector added, "I am speaking to you alone now because I was informed that you have the power to reach large amounts of people to believe a certain way through your ability to write. Certain people in your country's government, this country's government and the country to the east know of my existence. That means that many other people will most likely know soon. It is only a matter of time before thousands and then millions will know that I am here. When that occurs, I will probably go into hiding somewhere else. I will take care of the settlers around the fell for as long as I can. However, my main objective is to protect the hammer pieces that I now have and to continue to search for the last remaining ones. You can protect my identity for a long time by writing my story as you have just witnessed."

Dan was now extremely confused. He was previously told not to write the truth. He asked, "Do you mean that you want me to write about everything?"

The Protector replied, "Because no average human would believe it. You must write it in such a way as not to be believed."

Dan then carefully asked, "So you want me to deliberately sabotage my news career by writing fiction to save you from being exposed to the world?"

The Protector just stared at him and walked quietly away. Dan stood there open-mouthed. Once he was able to collect his thoughts, he returned to the group. He went over to Andy and shook his hand saying, "Glad to see that you're alive Andy. Who else would I go to if I had any electrical questions?"

Andy laughed and said, "Ooh." The wound in his left side reminded him that it was there.

"When can we move you?" Dan asked. "And how soon can all of us leave?"

Balinn lightly grabbed Dan's arm and motioned to him to come with him into the next room. Once there, Balinn promptly said, "Your friend can never leave here. He was injured by Joulupukki's staff that contained a piece of the hammer. Its power has left a wound that will never heal if he were to leave this place. His only chance of survival is to stay with us under the care of the Protector. The hammer can cause death, but it can also preserve life. Say your parting words to your friend and then return to your own world."

Balinn left Dan without saying another word. He only nodded and disappeared into the dimly lit hallway. Dan stood still for a minute and then returned to Andy's side. Only Pete and Agents Washington and Torino were still there. Everyone else had already said their goodbyes. After the three others wished Andy their best, they each stepped back to let Dan say his last words. Dan didn't know Andy for too long and he felt that the two agents should be the last ones to speak to him. It was Andy who requested that he speak with Dan last.

Andy looked at Dan with a big grin and he began what would be their final conversation. "Somehow, I feel like I've known you for a decade." Dan's confusion was easily seen. Andy laughed. "Oh, I see that you don't know what the hell I'm talking about. You see, I've known your family for well over ten years. Your mom, dad, Rina and I have had a professional relationship due to my line of work and their companies' contracts with our government. They couldn't tell you because of the nature of our dealings. They told me all about you and what a great writer you are. Your dad had strongly recommended that we try to get you to Finland by hook or by crook."

Dan was both lost and overwhelmed. Why would his father want him here? He never wanted his son to be a writer. He took little interest in any part of his career. It didn't make sense.

Dan conveyed this to Andy and all Andy could do was laugh again. He replied, "That's not why your father suggested that you be the one to do a story on this place. He wanted to give your career a boost and some recognition that he believed you deserved. He feels that you're a talented reporter who's stuck in a job at a dead-end newspaper. Besides, he didn't know about the supernatural aspects of this place. He thought that this adventure was about us solving a strange but earthly phenomenon before the Russians could.

Andy continued, "Embedding you in with us for the ride had a sense of danger to it, but he and the rest of your family had no idea how much. He knows that your mouth gets you in trouble with your bosses just as it has with him, but that doesn't mean that he doesn't love you and isn't concerned about your future."

Dan was still in the dark about all of this and Andy sensed it. "Think about it Dan. If you go back to New York without anything truly amazing to report, your boss will break your stones, but you won't lose your job. Pete will vouch for you. He'll tell Roger Harbinger that he was mistaken and that he's at fault for asking Roger to send you out on a wild goose chase. Pete will likely get fired, but that's okay. Pete's real job is working for two governments. He'll just move on and find another position as a cover. If you write a fluff piece about how Santa really lives in Finland with made-up details about the fell and the 'cute' elven tonttus, you'll get ridiculed by serious journalists. But if you write about a warrior Father Christmas battling a horned demon and you include all of the real details about it and a few made up ones of your own, you'll have yourself a great novel of fantasy."

A smile came over Dan's face. He would write a creative novel of fiction. The details he would include would make people in the three countries' governments who knew about the Protector cringe, but he could make up other details that would most likely put a long-lasting delay in anyone else coming out and trying to figure out what actually went on around here. After all, nobody would believe the other-worldly events that he would include in his book. The Protector could continue to find the last pieces of the hammer puzzle. By the time his cover was blown, he could very well have moved on.

Andy continued with his sales pitch. "Tell Roger your plans about your novel and how you want him to help you publish. Then tell him that you will include his name in the story along with a great big thank you to him in the beginning of the book and you've got it made. Just do me and the other agents a favor. Don't use our real names. You don't want our possible deaths and maybe the deaths of family members to be on your conscience."

Dan agreed and he and Andy looked at each other with Dan reaching out for a handshake. Andy pulled him in for a manly hug. He let Dan go when his side's pain kicked in again and then he leaned back in the large chair. Dan backed away slowly, but then in an instant he turned and walked out of the room where the other three had gone.

The four of them were led down the hallway by a tonttu who had been waiting. Just as they were entering the main tunnel, they noticed a familiar large shadow standing in front of them. The

Protector motioned for the others to leave him and Dan alone. "I have made arrangements for you and your friends to rejoin the others on the surface. The search party that is currently looking for you has found all of your belongings and will eventually find our tunnels if you don't leave quickly."

Dan started walking to catch up with the others when he suddenly stopped and asked, "What's actually your real name?"

The Protector gave a slight smile and answered, "I go by many names. Now I can actually claim the title of Joulupukki that many people have already bestowed upon me." After an uncomfortable five second period of silence, Dan turned around in a hurried manner. As he took a few steps, he heard a thundering voice. "But you can call me Nick."

Dan turned his head to look back but nobody was there. He paused for a moment and then eventually rejoined the other eleven where they were led to the surface through a secret passage by a couple of armed tonttus. They walked towards the state-of-the-art helicopters that were powered by fuel cells and had been hovering for hours. Within minutes, they were reunited with the rest of the original thirty-four, both living and dead.

20

PARTING IS SWEET AND SOUR

ithin three hours, Dan was flown by a helicopter back to Pete's ancestral cabin. He said his goodbyes to Pete's cousins and to Pete, who was staying behind to check on his grandfather. Pete's days at *The Mob* were most likely over. Dan was able to talk to Rina and his mother on the phone. A conversation with his father would have to wait. It would be a long conversation.

Dan decided to spend a night in a hotel in Rovaniemi because of the timing of his flight. He thought that he might take in the festive atmosphere of the holiday season. After all, it was the capital city of Santa Claus. His plans never came to fruition. When he arrived in his room, he sat down to check his texts and phone calls. He wanted to see if Roger and especially Nancy had left him any messages. He never got the chance to explore the city. That night, he never got up from his seated position. The exhaustive nature of the last several days took its toll on him and his body was begging for sleep.

He woke up the next morning, still in yesterday's clothes. He got up, but was a little disoriented until he paused to get his thoughts in line. His disappointment about missing out in exploring the city was overshadowed by his urgency to make it to the airport. He showered, changed his clothes, packed, and grabbed a coffee and pastry from the continental breakfast downstairs. He hailed a taxi and headed for the airport. His hotel was only ten minutes from the airport and his urgent feelings of being late quickly subsided. The taxi dropped him off without any major traffic issues.

As Dan was about to enter the airport, he turned around and paused briefly to reflect on what he had witnessed and experienced. As he stared at the snow-covered surroundings and people moving about, he thought about how surreal everything was. He looked around and shook his head. These travelers had no idea what truly terrible things existed in this world. Of course, they knew about war, crime and poverty. What they didn't know was that there were supernatural forces also at play spreading evil; at first it was behind the scenes and buried in time for centuries, for an unknown reason, the evil returned then was destroyed. Or was it?

Dan wondered if it was really over. Would something else come to the surface and spread terror in Finland or somewhere else in the world?

He couldn't be sure, nor did he want to even think about it right now. He stepped back from his thoughts and walked inside the airport.

Dan was astonished when he saw Kirsti inside the terminal. Kirsti kissed him as soon as she saw him and said in a soft voice, "I hope you come back and visit me, uh, us, under better circumstances."

Dan nodded and with little hesitation, he quickly kissed her and nervously responded, "I will. And you can come to the States too."

They walked with each other for a while, both of them trying to keep this moment from ending. As they came to the end of the line for both, they wrapped their arms around one another. Kirsti began to cry. She looked up at him and whispered, "My cousins told me everything about what you did for me. I owe you my life and much more. Thank you. I will never forget what you did."

Dan, trying to shrug off the hero image, asked, "How is your grandfather?"

Kirsti said, "He had surgery immediately after he was flown to a hospital in Rovaniemi. It helped that he was loosely associated with our federal government. The surgery went well. He has a very long road to recovery."

"Well, he's a strong guy," Dan said.

"And stubborn too," Kirsti added with a slight laugh.

Dan smiled and nodded his head in agreement. They both looked nervously around before embracing one last time. They held onto each other for a few seconds and then Dan backed slowly away. He turned and began walking towards the baggage check counter, occasionally looking back to see if she was still there. She was, raising her left hand slightly every time he turned around. Eventually, he was at the check-in counter and then the gate. He was hoping his flight to Helsinki would be without anything unusual happening.

Fortunately, except for a fifteen-minute flight delay, his flight went off without any major hitches. Dan never even thought about whether he would be pestered by some kid or other lonely person on this flight; he'd bought out the three seats in his row. He simply settled into the furthest from the aisle seat, put in his air pods and leaned his head against the window. He fell asleep within minutes, interrupted briefly by announcements and takeoff. Overall, he engaged in the sleep of sleeps.

He awakened when the plane began its final descent into Helsinki. He exited rather quickly due to the mostly empty plane. He walked to where he was planning to wait until his next flight, but he was met by a man whose face was all too familiar to him.

Artemis Trent grabbed Dan's larger suitcase right out of his hand and without hesitation started walking away. "Follow me." Dan was too stunned to be able to muster up a response.

Trent walked rather quickly. Dan finally caught up to him and was about to ask a slew of questions, but the man opened a side door and encouraged Dan to exit. Soon they were outside and walking towards another plane. It was smaller than what he had just traveled on, probably a private charter. Dan thought Trent was bringing him to the whiz kid Ted Winters, but he quickly dismissed that idea due to Ted's preference for flying with the general public.

The aircraft was sleek looking, but had no distinguishable markings on the outside. It must be an MI6 junket, he thought as he walked up the stairs and entered a nicely adorned cabin that contained only about ten seats. There was a small dining area, a tiny kitchen and a couple of decent sized sofas.

He was led by Trent to the front row on the left side, which only had two seats. Trent stood in the aisle while Dan sat down. As Trent walked away, Dan saw his mysterious host slumped down in the window seat of the right front row. He did not recognize him. Dan tried not to stare, but he was trying to figure out who his host was. The stranger was looking intently out of the nearest window and Dan couldn't make out any facial features.

After a few moments, the stranger turned straight ahead and said, "I knew about it, but I couldn't stop it." Dan was rather surprised. It was Ted. He was half talking, half mumbling. Ted continued, "I saw it in my head, but I couldn't tell what it was."

Dan asked him, "What do you mean Ted? What did you see?" Dan sensed that something huge was about to be divulged to him because he guessed that it had something to do with Ted's special abilities.

Ted didn't answer. He just kept looking forward without hardly blinking. After several minutes of silence, the pilot announced that they would be taxiing to the runway momentarily. Dan sat back, buckled up and waited for take-off. It was an excruciating fifteen minutes until they were firmly in the air. When the jet leveled off, Dan tried to ease himself into a conversation with Ted by asking, "Why did you charter a private jet this time?"

Without looking at Dan, Ted said, "It's one of my parents' toys. I couldn't bear to be around people right now. I tracked where you were by having Artemis use some of his contacts. I was waiting for you in this jet for three days."

Dan uttered, "Wait. You've been sitting in a plane for that long waiting for me to show up? Why?"

Dan waited patiently for an answer. Ted finally composed himself long enough to spit out a series of seemingly non-connected sentences which included the words, "I tried to use my foresight. The American, British, Canadian, German and French governments wanted me to look hard into my subconscious. I could see it, but I couldn't explain what I was seeing. It's too late. Millions will suffer."

Dan tried to piece together Ted's puzzle. He deduced that Ted was talking about a vision that he had. It was either that or a situation existed in the world, which prompted the U.S. government and its allies to contact Ted about using his unique talents. Obviously, what Ted eventually saw terrified him. It was made worse by the fact that he couldn't give them a clear picture, especially since it sent him into a form of shock. Realizing that he was no longer of any use to them, they likely sent him on his way without so much as trying to calm his nerves. Dan guessed that Ted sought him out because he had made some sort of connection with him, even though they hardly knew each other. Ted didn't try to speak for the duration of the flight.

Artemis asked, "Mr. Becket. Can I get you anything?"

Dan said, "No thanks. I'm good."

That was the only conversation until the jet landed at JFK. After the pilot brought the craft to a final stop, he announced that they could deplane at any time. Ted didn't move. Dan stood up and walked to the aisle. He looked at Ted and said, "Hey Ted. If you want to talk, just call me. I wish I could help you and I will, when you're ready to let me into that mind of yours.

Dan walked to the door. His bags were waiting with Trent. They looked at each other and gave a polite nod. This was the warmest Trent had been to him. As Dan was about to walk out the already opened door, Ted called out, "Dan!" Dan turned around and before he could say anything, Ted spoke again. "When I first met you a week or so ago, I said that I was on a trip to Iceland. I was actually going to a secret location in China to speak with officials and scientists from many countries. I saw something in my mind and I told my parents. They called my school headmaster, who actually works for our government. He got my parents in contact with a man by the name of Joe Archer."

That guy Archer is into everything, Dan thought. Ted continued, "The next thing I knew, I was off to Iceland where my parents were and then on to China."

Dan stood at the door and waited for Ted to continue. When Ted appeared to look out the window, Dan assumed the conversation to be over. He again turned towards the door. He had already stepped outside and Trent was about to close the door when Ted, now kneeling on his seat, called out, "Dan, I don't know what to do about these letters that I keep seeing in my mind!"

Dan put his hand on the closing door, leaned in and asked, "What letters?"

Ted paused, took a deep breath and spelled out, "n-C-o-V." Dan had no idea what those letters meant. Trent was getting anxious due to Ted's apparent meltdown.

He looked at Dan and said, "Mr. Beckett. Mr. Winters is very upset right now. Let's give him some time to relax. We will call you if Mr. Winters needs to speak to you."

Dan once again attempted to keep the door open. When he was about to ask more questions, Trent slammed the door shut.

Dan looked out over the airport tarmac and then descended to the bottom of the stairs. A car was waiting for him, probably ordered by Trent. As he got in and sat down, he looked at the jet and thought to himself, this year will go down in history. I wonder what next year will bring?

21

Even though Dan was planning to go straight home and hit the sheets, the driver had other ideas. He brought him to the doorstep of *The Mob*. Somehow, Roger Harbinger knew of Dan's exclusive travel accommodations and sent out a driver to meet him. Dan quickly went to his Uber App and ordered his own transportation. He told the driver that he wasn't leaving the vehicle. The driver had obviously communicated to Roger that they were downstairs because within about three minutes, Roger was there tapping on Dan's window. He refused to roll it down, but the driver did. "Traitor." Dan said to him as the driver shrugged his shoulders.

Roger shouted, "You made me come all the way down here to get you! I want to speak to you right now!" He calmed down a bit. "You didn't answer any of my phone calls." Dan tried to interrupt, but Roger went on and on. "Dan, you had better have some kind of a story because you are walking on thin ice."

"Thin ice," Dan said in a low voice. "If he only knew."

When Roger took a breather from all of his ranting, Dan noticed that a car that was probably his Uber ride had pulled up in front of them. He grabbed his bags, threw an unnecessary tip to the driver and got out of the car. Roger, thinking Dan had finally come to his senses, stepped back to give Dan room to move. Dan walked up to Roger and said, "Hello Roger. It's good to see you too. Did you miss me? I will have a story for you and then some. But right now, I'm going home to my cozy apartment, a nice warm bed and my funny looking rodent of a dog. I'll see you."

Before Roger could say anything more, Dan opened the door to his new ride and was off. He asked the driver to stop and he rolled down the window. He yelled something to Roger, but Roger couldn't hear him. Roger yelled back, "What? What did you say?"

Dan leaned nearly halfway out of his window and yelled again, "Merry Christmas Roger! I hope Santa brings you everything you deserve!" The car sped off and an astonished Roger watched it disappear down the street.

Traffic was thick and the ride took a little longer than expected, but Dan didn't mind. He was home. He was back in the city that he loved. Soon he would be in his apartment sipping bourbon and holding the only living creature who truly understood him, his little rat dog. He texted his neighbor Nancy hours before that he would be by to pick FB up, but there was no response. He tried again when the Uber arrived, but she still didn't respond.

It didn't bother him. She was probably out walking the dog or running a few miles.

The car pulled up in front of Dan's building. Within a few minutes, Dan was on his floor and knocking on Nancy's door. When there was no answer, he headed to his apartment. He briefly juggled his keys and unlocked the door. Upon opening it, he was greeted by FB, Nancy and a decorated apartment. "Surprise!" Nancy exclaimed. "Welcome back." FB jumped into his arms. Nancy walked over to him and gave him a small kiss and a hug. Dan at first thought it to be awkward, but he enjoyed it nonetheless.

After the initial shock, he looked around and saw a small tabletop Christmas tree, fully decorated. There was garland covering the length of his fireplace mantle and a string of colored lights outlining the frame of his door.

Dan said to her, "Looks great. It really does. Thank you. I think that this is the first time that I've had a tree in over a decade. I hope that you didn't go through too much trouble."

Nancy responded, "It was no bother. I did it this morning after you first texted that you were on your way home. Everyone should have a Christmas tree, including you." Dan smiled and after an excruciating few seconds of silence, Nancy spoke again. "Well, I've got to get back to work. With tomorrow being Christmas Eve and all, I want to have a clear slate for the next couple of days." As Nancy passed by him, she squeezed his hand and gave him another little kiss on the cheek.

That was two kisses in two minutes, Dan thought. Was Nancy taking this platonic relationship to a different level? He stumbled out some words. "Let me walk you out." He put FB down and followed her into the hallway. He stopped as she continued to her door, which was about twenty feet away from his. Before she could unlock her door, Dan uttered, "Hey."

She replied, "Hey yourself."

Dan laughed. "No. I mean uh, are you doing anything tomorrow night?" Dan knew that she didn't have any family nearby.

She looked at him as she put her key in her door. With a slight grin she asked him, "Daniel Becket, are you asking me out on a date? A real date?"

He responded with a question. "Well, if I was, would you go?"

Nancy liked this little game, so she came back with, "Maybe."

Dan started backing up towards his open door and asked, "Maybe?"

Nancy stepped into her apartment, leaned out and said, "Why not." Then she leaned back in and closed her door.

Dan turned to face the inside of his apartment and looked in to see FB in a sitting position staring up at him. Dan bent slightly down, looked at the little dog and said, "Why not?" Then he took his right foot and closed the door.

Daniel Becket returns

in

COLD DARK KNIGHTS